SAGACIOUS TEENS

SAGACIOUS TEENS
The Wisdom of Today's Teenagers

J. THOMPSON

SAGACIOUS TEENS
THE WISDOM OF TODAY'S TEENAGERS

iUniverse books may be ordered through booksellers or by contacting:

iUniverse LLC
1663 Liberty Drive
Bloomington, IN 47403
www.iuniverse.com
1-800-Authors (1-800-288-4677)

ISBN: 978-1-4917-4366-9 (sc)
ISBN: 978-1-4917-4368-3 (hc)
ISBN: 978-1-4917-4367-6 (e)

Printed in the United States of America.

iUniverse rev. date: 08/27/2014

Dedicated To
My parents, Julius and Louise

Acknowledgements

First, I thank and praise God for everything! Second, I was blessed with a father who encouraged perseverance and discipline and a mother who taught me the joy of reading and living. Third, I am grateful for the kind words from my sister Alice, the encouragement from friends, and the motivation from the entire IUniverse editorial staff. Lastly, I have been fortunate to be in the people of many wise young people of whom the following stories are based.

HAUNTED HOUSE

[Act 1: Scene 1 – Booth at a neighborhood fast-food restaurant. Time – directly after school around 4pm. Carlos and Ernesto are sipping drinks.]

Carlos – We had so much fun in Ms. Alcorn's class the other day.

Ernesto – Man, I love her class. I think that I love her too. She makes everything so interesting.

Carlos – Yep. She told us to write a story for English class. It could have been something that really happened or something imaginary.

Ernesto – What did you write about that was so much fun?

Carlos – She told us that we could work in pairs or work alone. I chose Antonio for my partner because he is a great artist and I could use him for my illustrations. Plus he's got a great imagination so he could add tidbits to my story.

Ernesto – So what was story about?

Carlos – It was about a stoned-out party last Saturday.

Ernesto – Where was it?

Carlos – Hey, you know you're my homie but this kind of happened spontaneously. It happened so fast, like a SST jet, no, more like warp speed in a Star Trek movie. [pause] I was walking my dog ....

Ernesto – You mean that ugly pug.

Carlos – Hey, my pug is valuable. That dog is worth over a grand.

Ernesto – More like a grand of pennies.

Carlos – Whatever! My dog had to take a leak. He got away from me and ran to the back of this old, abandoned house. The house was boarded up; it was one those HUD foreclosure homes. It had all of its windows and doors boarded up. As I walked around the back of the house, looking for Skip, I noticed one window with a loose board. I pried the board loose and there was an open window, no glass or anything. I looked in. My dog looked in too. I told him to sit down while I jumped in the window.

Ernesto – Man, you entered a broken-down house. Isn't that against the law?

Carlos – What do you mean? Nobody lived there.

Ernesto – Dude, that's called criminal trespassing. That house was boarded up by the police or the sheriff. That house is owned by HUD; that's the government authority of Housing and Urban Development. You were trespassing on federal property and you could have been arrested and got five years in prison.

Carlos – Where do you get this stuff?

Ernesto – Hey, I look at TV. I look at cop shows, FBI shows, and other reality shows.

Carlos – Well, I was caught up in the zone. I saw this house. I peeked in. I went in the basement window and walked around. Man, it was so clean! I mean it was totally cleaned out. There was nothing there. No junk. No furnace. No furniture. Nothing! There wasn't even any dirt or dust.

Ernesto – I see why you were intrigued. It's like when Sherlock Holmes gets bit by an investigative bug. It's like curiosity was getting the best of you.

Carlos – Yeah, and an idea occurred to me. I called a couple of folks. Then they called a couple of folks. I called you but your phone was zonked out.

Ernesto – My money must have been funny that month.

Carlos – I feel you. I told folks that we needed four boom-boxes with plenty of fresh batteries. My mom has one of those emergency flashing lanterns. I asked others to bring some type of emergency lighting that runs on batteries. I didn't want to mess around with candles. I told everybody to bring the chicks, the chips, the chug-a-lug, and some cush. This wasn't planned in advance. It was automatic. Man, we had a jukin' session in about an hour that was out of this world. We partied like there was no tomorrow. Like that song, we partied like it was 1999.

Ernesto – Doggone it. I missed out.

Carlos – Yep. Well, time passed. We had fun. But when the drinks were running low or when they were all gone, somebody said that we better split. Somebody then went to the window, but it was all boarded up. It didn't make any sense. I looked at all the windows and they were boarded up too. I was stoned out but I remember where the window was when we first entered the building. I couldn't figure out how it got closed off. Like, we entered through here, yet it didn't make sense. People started to freak out. They said, "What's going on? Are we going to be buried alive?" I said, "No way, this is just some fluke. Maybe the wind blew some lumber over the window. All we need to do is knock the wood away and get out."

Ernesto – But if the wind blew the lumber over the window, why didn't your dog just bark? He must really be a good-for-nothing mutt.

Carlos – Skip wasn't there. I dropped him off home because some of the girls were scared of him and I had to pick up the lantern and other things from the house. I told the guys that all we needed to do was kick the boarded up window out. I then realized that the window was about four feet above the ground. So I couldn't just kick my way out. I tried to push it out and then hit it with my fist. My God, lumber hurts when you hit it with your bare hands. As I was pounding on the wood, a voice said in a deep, baritone type of way, "Cease!" [*pause*] I stopped and looked around. [*pause*] I again hit on the wood. Again a voice said "Cease!" I told everybody to stop playing around. This was no joking matter. All the chicks and dudes looked at me weird. I punched on the wood over the window, over and over again, and then the voice said "Cease! Cease!"

I looked at my crew and they said, "Hey man, nobody over here said anything." People were getting freaked out. They admitted to hearing the voice also. Somebody said, "Are we going to be buried alive?" I said, "No way. We are just going to have to take turns pounding away." One chick said that she was going to call her boyfriend. That was funny because she was *real* friendly with two different hard-legs at the party earlier. She pulled out her phone but the call didn't go through.

Other people got worried and pulled out their cell phones. Another chick said that she was going to call her dad. He was a cop. We tried to talk her out of it because that would incriminate all of us. She said that she didn't care. She said, "What's going to happen? They might send us up to juevie for a year or do some community service in the hood. I just don't want to die. I don't want to be buried alive."

Well her phone didn't work either. It was like we were in a dead zone; you know those places on earth where there is no cell phone reception. It was like being at the tip of the North Pole or at the bottom of the Grand Canyon. Everybody tried to call and not one phone worked.

Other guys tried to pry the window boards open, and when they pounded and pried the boards or made any kind of noise, the voice said, "Cease! Cease!" I was so scared. It was like a nightmare. Chicks were shivering and whimpering. Heck, some dudes were shaking and crying too. Nobody knew what to do. We kept looking at each other for answers and everyone's faces were blank.

Some people tried to blame me, but I threw that right back in their own faces. I told them that no one forced them to come along. It's a free country. This is America. They all freely and willingly came on a voluntary basis.

That got them off my back for a while. Then people started to fall asleep. First, it was just one or two people dozing off. Then I noticed a couple more sleeping. One guy was snoring. I think that there was a shortage of oxygen. The air was getting thin. The heavier people were the first to fall asleep.

I feared that we would all suffocate and die in our sleep. I was determined not to go out like this. I was frantic. I needed to figure out a way out. Then all of a sudden, I remembered. When Skip was a puppy, he would always explore the neighborhood. He couldn't jump over the fence so he would dig in a spot every day until he could scoot up under the fencing. His motto must be, "If you can't jump over it, or go through it, then go around it or under it". I remembered that little puppy scooting under the fence and running away from home. He would always come back but I learned a lot from him.

I told the remaining healthy people that we needed to dig or our lives would cease to exist. We had to find a spot where there was loose foundation. We needed to dig first to get some fresh air. Then we needed to dig deep enough so that at least one of us could scoot out and get help for the rest of us.

Ernesto – So you are telling me that you *actually* tried to dig your way out?

Carlos – It wasn't at all easy. First, we had to find some dirt or a loose brick. The lower parts of a building are where the foundation lies. The foundation is usually made of concrete, sometimes concrete blocks or just slabs of cement. There is usually no dirt. But I didn't realize that until I realized we were trapped. The door leading up to the upper level, probably the kitchen of the house, was securely boarded. I searched the basement for a way out. Fortunately, I couldn't believe it, but there was some type of door. It was like a trap door about 4 X 4 feet. I opened the door and there was a dirt floor. Perhaps this was where there was once a coal bin years ago.

Ernesto – A coal bin?

Carlos – Yeah, about a hundred years ago people would heat their houses with coal. Today, we mainly heat our houses up with natural gas. Back then, a coal truck would drop chunks of coal off at the house by means of a chute. Today, we have natural gas pipelines. Well, I opened this small door. I felt a dirt floor beneath me. It was dark, ugly, and stinking. I think that there were dead snakes and rats in there. I didn't care. All I thought about was escaping. Digging wasn't easy. Digging on your hands and knees with bare hands is no joke. We had no other choice; no other alternative. Like I said earlier, the entire basement of the house was a concrete slab. This was our only hope. Digging with your hands is tedious. A shovel or even a spoon would have helped. I got others to take turns. After we dug for about an hour, I felt some type of breeze, a little fresh air, seeping in. I was so relieved. I literally placed my head in the dirt so I could breathe in some fresh air for a few seconds. I immediately called out for help. I didn't care about the police. I didn't care about juvie. I just did not want to die. [*pause*] (Carlos catches his breath)

And guess who came to our rescue?

Ernesto – I can't imagine. Who?

Carlos – Skip. My pug. I had taken him home, but he must have used his psychic animal powers or instincts to realize my misfortune. I left him at the house, but somehow he knew something was wrong and came looking for me. He probably got out of the house the way he normally does. When I called out for help, Skip started barking. When we first started partying, he didn't sense any real danger then. I mean, we were just having fun. But hours later, when I started banging on the wood at the window, Skip must have sensed danger, left home, and decided to come to my rescue. Well, he just kept yapping until a neighbor came by, wondering what all the noise was about. The neighbor heard my calls for help and notified the police. When the police arrived, they pried the boards away from the windows, helped us to exit the building, and I confessed to my wrongdoings. The sick went in the ambulance and went directly to the hospital. The rest of us had to answer questions first before the police took us in a paddy wagon to the hospital for a checkup. The police officers didn't believe in the haunted house story and the mysterious voice.

Ernesto – What did the police believe in then?

Carlos – Their theory was that someone must have noticed that we entered the house; then probably an hour after we entered, realizing that we were getting high and having fun, they secretly boarded up the window that we had first entered. They had to do it slowly and stealthily, not to arouse suspicion. Perhaps they were rival gangbangers. Perhaps it was a crazy adult. Anyway, the police said they were dusting the area for prints and other incriminating evidence. Whoever boarded up the window can be charged with attempted murder. This was no simple prank.

Ernesto – Wow! That was something else.

Carlos – And I'm sorry that I did it. I was only sentenced to one year of community service, but I now have a lifetime sentence related to a fear of basements and claustrophobia.

Ernesto – Man, was this story real or made up?

Carlos – You decide for yourself. Keep in mind that Ms. Alcorn's writing assignment could have been from something real or imaginary.

Bad Boys

[Act I: Scene 2. *The same afternoon in the restaurant at another booth. Richard and Robert are sharing French fries.*]

Richard – Man my girl is sweating me.

Robert – What's up?

Rich – She says I don't listen to her. She wants me to stop hanging out with my boys and to spend quality time with her.

Rob – What does she mean by "quality time'? That sounds like a divorced couple deciding on how much time each parent should spend with each child. *[pause. Robert is munching on some fries.]* She just wants to drive a wedge between you and your boys. She's selfish. She wants you all to herself. She wants a chump to go shopping with her, talk on the phone all day, go for long walks, have romantic dinners, wash and wax her car, and then maybe give up a little sex.

Rich – I guess that I didn't see it totally that way, but deep down I did get that feeling. I do all I can for her, but I need time to myself, for myself, to regroup and reenergize.

Rob – Well you can't let a girl drain you. They will drain you both physically and emotionally if you let them. I think you know what I mean about a physical drain. Remember, they are on the receiving end.

Rich – I get you.

Rob – Emotionally, you have to make a stand. You have to stand up for yourself. You can't be whipped. You know what I mean by "whipped", right?

Rich – Heck, I'm not sex-whipped. I mean she is good, probably the best, but I have self-confidence. I, too, am the best she ever had.

Rob – That's exactly what I'm talking about. So why should you give in to her every wish. She snaps her finger and you are supposed to jump. If you ask how high, she's ready to put you down or berate you for asking. You aren't supposed to ask how high, just keep jumping until she is satisfied. Why should you be the super-chump? Be a man. Make a stand. If she can't deal with it, then cool, move on, find another chick. They're plenty at school and hundreds in the hood.

Rich – Yeah, you remind me of Slim.

Rob – You mean the 350lb football player on the varsity team.

Rich – Yeah, I'm referring to him. He told me once that women are a dime a dozen. Don't sweat them. If one doesn't act right, there are eleven more itching to roll in the hay with you if you have the right stuff.

Rob – Yeah, but if you do find the right woman, don't mess around. Stick with that one like super glue. But in this case you need to tell your woman that you need some space. You need to relax and regroup. Tell her that you plan to be a better man after that.

Rich – I like that 'better man pitch', but what if she doesn't buy it? What if she thinks that it is just a ruse to break off the relationship?

Rob – Then so be it. A man has to have time to hang out with his boys. We talk football, baseball, basketball and more. We talk about the players, the coaches, and the team owners. When players make decisions to move to another city, it's a strategic move. The days are long gone when the managers and owners call all the shots. Today's players have serious input. The great legends in the day were subservient to their masters. Don't misinterpret my words. They did the best that they could under the circumstances. They made good money, but many of their contracts sucked, compared to today's standards. Ten years ago the best players made most of their money off endorsements from major companies. Today, players are making money on playing the game, contracts, commercials, endorsements, and starting their own businesses. Man, they're entrepreneurs! Some go to college and others postpone college while they are in their peak. Tomorrow is not promised. One injury can ruin you. Women don't realize how important these types of conversations are to us. This is how *real* men connect with each other. We only have 24 hours a day. We go to school. Most of us work after school to pay for our rides and to have money to take the chicks out. We have to feel like men at times and not just be robots performing duties for them.

Rich – That's so true. Women don't realize that when we are talking about the superstars we are also connecting their lives to our own. Like you said, one personal injury can devastate and ruin their future. One sexual rendezvous can change their life. The same holds for us. We learn from their actions. We can avoid mistakes after witnessing their mistakes.

Rob – I hear you. We have seen superstars' lives change because of one close encounter with the other species.

Rich – Women are of the same species as men. I think they call it homo-sapiens.

Rob – I beg to differ. Scientifically, we both have blood, hearts, lungs, etc. But deep down, I believe that they truly came from another planet.

Rich – Oh, like that old theory that women came from Venus and men came from Mars?

Rob – Yep. I mean women totally think differently from men.

Rich – But that's natural. Opposites attract. Remember in our Physics class the teacher was talking about polar opposites and we experimented with magnets. Something about the force fields that have to be dissimilar to get a reaction. Well men and women are different and that is what attracts us to them and them to us.

Rob – Well, you need to man up. You can't just be a robot or a boy-toy for her. Take time to hang out with your boys.

Rich – You give good advice, like that TV doctor who helps people with relationships. He's so cool. They even call him by his first name on TV. He's not hung up or stuck up on titles. He's down to earth.

Rob – Just like me. I call them like I see them. Heck, I'll send you the bill!

(Carlos and Berra then join Robert and Richard in the booth.)

Carlos – What's up?

Rich – Nothing much. We were just talking about relationships. Sometimes when a girl is sweating you, you then have to chill, give her some space or just move on.

Berra – I agree. That's why I keep a half-a-dozen or more chicks in tow. *(Berra, often referred to as Bear because he is huge, then pulls out his phone and smiles.)*

Carlos – [*Emphatically*] Let me see. [*Carlos then snatches Bear's phone from him.*]

Berra – Man, give me back my phone! [*Carlos evades Bear and searches the phone's contacts.*]

Carlos – Let's call one of them.

Bear – Give me back my phone. My women are too busy. They don't have time to talk right now.

Carlos – All of them? You're saying that all of your women are busy right now. Get outta here! You don't have any real women. You only have make-believe.

Bear – Man, my women are for real. I got almost a dozen. They're just busy now.

Carlos – How could six or more women all be busy after 4 in the afternoon. I saw the names of at least 20.

Bear – They're in school. They're at work. They don't have time to talk. I schedule my talks after school. They have little brothers and sisters to babysit after school and other important things to do.

Carlos – Then let's text somebody. They can easily return a text message regardless of what they might be doing.

Bear – I'm not doing that! I don't have to prove anything to you or to anybody else.

Carlos – You're not getting any butt.

Bear – Man, I got a daughter. Be for real.

Carlos – Just having a daughter doesn't mean you are getting any butt. It only means that you used to get laid.

Bear – I got my share of hoes.

Rob – Man, anybody can get some hoes. They got $5 and $10 ones a block away from school.

Carlos – Feel me! I'm talking about real women, not hoes; somebody that you're not ashamed of. Someone you can take home to momma.

Bear – Dude, I got real women, not hoes.

Carlos – Then what are their names? You don't even have names listed in your phone directory. You just have initials like "K" or "L" and other letters from the alphabet.

Bear – That's to be discreet so motherhubbards like you don't call and harass them.

Carlos – Yeah, yeah, yeah. I bet you have some grammar school babies. You probably got some sixth graders.

Bear – Man, I'm not a pedophile. I'm not a cradle snatcher.

Carlos – Nope, you're probably right about that. You nothing but an "imaginest".

Bear – That's not even a word.

Carlos – Maybe, maybe not, but one thing for sure is that you're not a playa.

Bear – I ought to kick your butt for dissing me. I know who I am and what I am. I don't need *you* to justify my existence.

Carlos – Probably all you can do is kick butt 'cause you're sure as heck not getting any butt.

[Carlos and Berra begin to scuffle. They look like old sparring partners in a boxing ring. Neither one is trying to hurt the other. Even though they are not throwing any real punches, this playful display of machismo might evolve into a real bloody match.]

Bear – Whatever! You have a right to your stupid opinion. Stupid is as stupid does. You're like that teacher I had in eighth grade. She tried to make me feel dumb and stupid. I ignored her stupid butt. I graduated on time! I don't let people define me – I define myself. Negative people like you are like bullies - always trying to force your opinions and thoughts on others.

Carlos – I'm not a bully. I'm a realist. You live in an imaginary world!

Bear – And you are a mental bully. But it's not going to work on me. If I succumb to your manipulations, those bullying tactics, then I'm a wimp. It'll be my fault. The harder you hit, the more you attack me, only makes me stronger and wiser. You'll see. When the prom comes up, I'll have two chicks, one on each arm. I don't have to prove anything to you now.

Carlos – Yeah, and I bet that they'll both be blow-up dolls.

Bear – You know nothing about my personal life, so you imagine what you can't see. If I allow you to brainwash me with your nonsense, it would be the same as me bullying up myself. I heard it was called self-bullying destructive behavior.

Carlos – That's not even a word. That's about as lame as your pretend women. You have to pretend that you have women and now you're creating pretend words to justify your lame life.

Bear – Self-bullying is real. I went to one of those workshops on assertiveness training. The counselor explained it well. She said that bullies pick on weak people. They say negative stuff about them all day long. After a while, the victims believe the bullies. For example, they might say that a person is ugly or stupid. After a while, the victims begin to believe that they are actually ugly or stupid. This is reinforced by a crowd or mob who supports the bully's accusations. The bully calls you ugly, then everybody in the class calls you ugly, and after a while you begin to believe that you are *really* ugly and start looking in the mirror and wondering why you are so ugly. This is so reprehensible because prior to ever meeting this bully, no one ever called you ugly. In fact, you look better than some movie stars, but what the bully has done is brainwash you into believing what he wants you to believe. Then you incorporate his philosophy into your psyche. You start bullying yourself with negative thoughts. Some people go so far as committing acts of violence and even suicide.

Carlos – Wow! That *is* sick.

Bear – Yes it is. That is why I am not going to let sick people like you make me sick. It's like a disease - a contagious disease that spreads and spreads. Somebody has a cold or the flu and they spread their germs around. I'm not going to let you infect me with your negativity.

Carlos – Hey man, I apologize. I'm sorry. I didn't realize the full extent of my actions.

Berra – Apology accepted. We can't let our friendship end over one or two misconceptions.

Richard – Man, this was enlightening! I'm not going to let my chick bully or brainwash me either. I knew something was up with her. Now I'm convinced. I'm going to take a stand. Stand up for my convictions. If she can't deal with it, then I'll be stepping.

Rob – You see, it pays to hang around me. Learn something new every day.

[They both chuckle.]

Broke

[Act I: Scene 3. Carmelita and Rachel enter the restaurant and sit at another booth.]

Carmelita – My boyfriend is always broke and I feel like he's just using me.

Rachel – Do you love him?

Carmelita– I love him with my whole heart. He was my first, my only, and I hope my last.

Rachel – But you don't know if he's the best. I mean, compared to the rest.

Carmelita – How many boys are in America my age? Millions? I don't have to date thousands of guys to justify my feelings for Rob. I know that he's the best. He's the best for me. He makes me feel so special. When we talk, he listens. So many boys talk and don't seriously listen. They can barely wait for you to finish a sentence before they're interrupting you with *their* thoughts. For some people, a conversation is like a tennis match. One side serves the ball and the opponent receives it and immediately reacts. But Rob listens intently to my ideas and problems. It's like he hangs on every word.

Rachel – Ok, so he's a good listener, but he's always broke?

Carmelita – Yeah, nothing is perfect. I mean most girls would want a sensitive man who listens. What I mean is that most boys just talk about what interests them. They are self-centered. But not Rob. He can just look at me with those big brown inquisitive eyes and those lovely thick eyelashes. I can tell him some of my darkest secrets.

Rachel – I see.

Carmen – And he looks into my eyes when I talk. I mean the whole time. It's like he's in rapt attention. There's something to be said when someone continually looks into your eyes. It's like connecting with your soul. It's mysterious. Most people look away, avert their eyes, or look at their watch or phone, but not Rob, he looks at me intently and truly listens to my every word.

Rachel – Wow, like a psychiatrist?

Carmen – Exactly, but even better. He makes me feel so good inside. He looks directly into my eyes when I talk. I mean the whole time. It's like he's attentive to every word and phrase that I say. My words are like food for thought. It's mysterious. When I talk to Rob, it's like heaven. It's like unloading a heavy burden. It's like going to a confessional booth and spilling your guts out to a priest. You feel so relieved after that. It's almost like good sex.

Rachel – How could talking be like sex?

Carmen – I don't know how to explain it, but when he listens and I reveal my innermost self to him, I'm talking about my soul, it's like I just opened my brain or mind, he entered, and rivers of gushy, emotional baggage flowed out.

Rachel – You are saying that he touched your soul? How could that be? What was it like?

Carmen – I can't adequately put it into words but my soul *was* touched. How do I know? I can't prove it. I cannot offer up scientific evidence of my soul encounter with this man, but I know it happened. It's something deep down. It's not really a feeling like an emotion. It's like you can feel your inner core. It's like digging into the Earth with a special machine and reaching the core of our planet. It's like all facades and outward expressions of materialism are meaningless when confronted with your soul.

Rachel – Well then maybe that's the key. You said that he's always broke. Maybe being broke got him in touch with his soul and then he can then connect with your soul. I mean, everybody else is thinking about buying the latest cell phones, jeans, shoes, watches, etc. If he's always broke, and if he spends his time focusing on his soul, contemplating and meditating then maybe he is introspective. He can see hidden things inside of himself and others. Consequently if he is in a relationship with you, then he wants to, or has to, connect with your soul.

Carmen – That's deep. Thanks. That's why I like talking to you. You help me get things into perspective. But the problem still remains – his finances. He works everyday but he is always broke. If I want to go out to dinner, he wants to get a frozen dinner for a dollar.

Rachel – Are you serious? A dollar?

Carmen – Dead serious! Or if I insist on going out, then he takes me to the local fast-food restaurant and orders one item from the dollar menu. Instead of soda pop, he insists that regular water from the fountain or faucet is healthier for you. Instead of fries, he talks about the sodium, cholesterol, and fat intake consumed from eating fried potatoes. If I mention a milkshake, he goes on and on about the calorie intake from the sugar and fats present in the drink. He talks about diabetes and high cholesterol.

Rachel – Wow, so you end up with a dollar burger or chicken nuggets?

Carmen – That's it. Instead of going out to the movies, he wants to look at television. If I insist on seeing a new release, guess what he does?

Rachel – Beats me.

Carmen – He will go to the dollar Red Box and rent the movie if it's out, otherwise we'll just have to wait.

Rachel – Wow – big spender! A whole dollar on a movie!

Carmen – Now you see my dilemma. There was a movie I just had to see. Everybody was talking about it at school. I know how Rob feels about spending $15 or more for the theatre. So I just treated him.

Rachel – (*sarcastically*) - You embarrassed him and he came up with the money?

Carmen – Did Hell just freeze over? No, I did not treat him in the sense of putting him down. I treated him to the movies. I bought the tickets; well I really gave him the money while we were in the car so he wouldn't be embarrassed.

Rachel – Or perhaps *you* wouldn't be embarrassed. How would it look if people saw you paying for the tickets at the movie theater? They might say that he's pimpin' you.

Carmen – Well, that's why I'm always discreet. Sometimes I want things, but then I have to always dish out the money. If I want to go to a fancy restaurant, I have to pay. It's not like he's trying to pimp me, he just doesn't have a dime. If he had it, then he would spend it on me, but he's always dead broke.

Rachel – Maybe he's spending it on another girl.

Carmen – No way. I thought of that initially. I did my investigative work. He's not seeing anyone else, and if he is, they are paying to play.

Rachel – Maybe he's just saving his money for some major purchase – like a car or a house.

Carmen – Nope, the boy is on drugs. Well, both drugs and alcohol.

Rachel – Are you certain? Do you have proof?

Carmen – Yes and yes.

Rachel – Well if he loves drugs and alcohol so much, then that explains why he is always broke. Those needs will never be fulfilled. They say the more you drink, the more you want to drink. That goes for drugs also. The body gets used to one high and seeks another high. You have to figure out a way to get him help.

Carmen – I know, but he won't talk about it. He won't go to a counselor. He brushes me off with the phrase, "Everybody has problems".

Rachel – Well then the only alternative is for you to leave him. You have to break it up because it's breaking you up inside.

Carmen – Yeah, but I can't live without him. Like I said earlier, his soul has touched my soul. I never felt like this before. Sexually, he was my first. That's another feeling. The way that he can compassionately listens to my every word and can interpret my unsaid thoughts. It's phenomenal. It's like I can't live with him and I can't live without him.

Rachel – Then maybe I'm wrong. You both need help and *you* need it the most.

Be Kind

[Act I: Scene 4. Lighting now focuses on Tina and Padma who are seen sitting at another booth in the restaurant.]

Tina – I have to break up with Rob.

Padma – Why? Girl, he is so fine. Tell me his weakness, his problems, and his faults. I don't mind picking up your rejects. Just like hand-me clothes. You can hand him down to me. After you kick him to the curb, I'll just dust him off and make him shine and be mine.

Tina – You can have him. He's too cruel. I can't live with anybody like him anymore. He works my last nerve.

Padma – All men are a trip. All of them work women's nerves. They think differently from us. You can't expect them to be compassionate and loving all the time. Women say that they want to make love all day long, but men only want to make love a few minutes in the sack.

Tina – I've never heard that before.

Padma – It's true. Women want to make love all day long. I'm not talking about sex, but real love. Women look for continuous expressions of love all day. It's like a guy asks to carry your books. That's an example of a caring love. He opens the door for you. He calls you twenty times a day.

Tina – I never thought of it like that but you're right. He is so loving and kind one minute, but then the next, he is so cold and calculating.

Padma – Hey, just deal with it or somebody else will. You can't expect men to think like women. Men aren't women. Their brains are wired differently. If you had a man that thought like a woman he would be gay. Then you wouldn't want him. He wouldn't want you either; he would want another man.

Tina – Yeah, you've made a good point but Rob is too cold and self-centered. He is downright selfish.

Padma – Aren't most men? I mean, at least those who don't have a bunch of kids. Rob is young, handsome, and smart. You can't expect him to be altruistic at his age. Now if he had a half of dozen bambinos, he would probably think of others before thinking of himself.

Tina – I see your point and it makes sense, but Rob makes me feel small. He makes me feel cheap.

Paddy – How can someone else make you feel small and cheap unless you already have those feelings deep inside of you?

Tina – He manipulates situations so that he is always happy. That's what I mean by selfish. For example, we plan to go out on a date. Let's say we plan to see a movie or go to a fancy restaurant. He will come to my house, scope me up and down, and if my clothes don't meet his standards, then I have to change.

Paddy – Well, some guys want their gals to look good when they're with them. It's an image thing. You are his girl. You represent him in public.

Tina – I don't represent anybody but myself! I am not one of his prized possessions. I'm not a trophy! I'm not a display item.

Paddy – Maybe you're overreacting.

Tina – Bull! One day I had on this cute pants suit. That didn't meet his approval. He wanted me to change and put on a mini-dress.

Padma – Well, come on now. A pants suit versus a mini-dress? He wanted to show you off. He wanted you to look sexy in public. That probably turned him on and later on, in the middle of the night, in the heat of passion; he would turn you on and out.

Tina – Please, sex is overrated. My feelings come first.

Padma – But he didn't take you to the store and buy you a dress that excited him. You had the outfit already in your closet. Evidently you liked wearing that mini-dress.

Tina – But that wasn't enough.

Padma – What else did he ask of you?

Tina – He didn't ask, he demanded that I take off my panties. He wanted me to look like a slut.

Padma – But you were with him. Nobody would say anything out of place.

Tina – You can't be too sure. Men would stare and ogle me. Women would gawk too. I would feel so cheap while he was feeling so good. A man, that is a *real* man, would be sensitive to a woman's feelings, but you see, he is *too* selfish. He only sees what he wants to see. He can't imagine my feelings. I felt like a trophy that he was showing off just for his personal enjoyment. I absolutely can't stand to be with him anymore.

Padma – Maybe you should have just spoken up. Men need to know how we feel. It's unfair to break up with someone if they don't know all the reasons or have an opportunity to rectify the situation. Relationships are a two-way affair.

Tina – I feel you, but this was just one more incident to add to a million others. This was the straw that broke this camel's back.

Padma – What else got on your nerves?

Tina – When it was time for a romantic dinner, or any lunch or dinner date for that matter, it was always his preference that had to be considered. If he had a taste for Chinese food, seafood, filet mignon, or anything, that's what we ate that day.

Padma – Many girls would love to have a boyfriend with good taste. Some guys just want hot dogs, burgers, or pizza.

Tina – Oh, he has a great taste in food. He has expensive tastes. He also loves healthy foods such as broiled fish and steamed vegetables.

Padma – That's very unusual. He sounds like the perfect man.

Tina – Are you being sarcastic? He is self-centered and manipulative. He never once cared about what I wanted to eat on any particular day. Sure, he had a great taste in foods, but he never considered my choices. The same was for entertainment. He was excited if the event interested him, but bored to death or simply refused to go to something that I suggested. The relationship was so one-sided. I just reached my limit. I was totally fed up when I text him that we should start seeing other people.

Padma – Again I say that you should have opened up and let him know of your preferences. Things could have been a whole lot worse. There are more serious problems in relationships other than what you have mentioned. And it irks me when people break up via the phone. Text messaging is so impersonal. You were in a committed relationship. You could have at least talked to him one-on-one, face to face.

Tina – Is that so? When it came to family, he was secretive about his. I allowed him to meet my parents, my brothers and sisters, my favorite uncle and aunt, and my grandparents. He, on the other hand, was reluctant for me to get close to anyone in his family. I met his sister once. We had a nice lunch together and we talked for hours. She is just the opposite of him. I talked to her that first time and it was if we had been knowing each other for years. Well, he put a damper on that because he made sure that I never saw or spoke to her again. When I asked him how he sister was, he would say that she was ok and then clam up, afraid to reveal any more information.

Padma – So you felt that he had something to hide.

Tina – Yeah, I mean family is family. You know what I mean. I wanted to get close to them so that I could get closer to him. Maybe he had another chick on the side and his family might bring up the other woman, unknowingly.

Padma- Maybe you're right. Maybe that's why he is so secretive. He doesn't want you to know his business. It seems that he had a reason for being so distant.

Tina – Yep, he was always distant, even when we were in the same room all by ourselves for a period of time. If we were at his crib looking at a movie, he would only look at the movie.

Padma – What's wrong with that?

Tina – I needed some communication, some type of interaction. When I view a flick, I'm always relating the action to something real in my life. I use movies as a way of learning as well as a form of entertainment. I don't just passively sit there. My mind is always in high-gear. And that's another thing. He was always in low-gear. He was always so laid-back; it was if nothing excited him.

Padma – Are you really saying that he never showed any emotion or excitement? If so, then I guess he was too boring.

Tina – Oh, he got excited about sex, but that was it. It was as if everything else was meaningless. I was beginning to feel like one of those plastic blow-up dolls waiting to be used and then cast aside until the next opportune moment.

Padma – I feel you.

Tina – When I look at a movie, I am always being critical and evaluative. I like to go to museums, roller-skating, shopping malls, concerts, parties, swimming, and long walks in the park. He likes to do nothing with me except eat at restaurants and lay up in the bed.

Padma – Well, he is a jock. All he thinks about is sports, sex, and self.

Tina – Correction. Get the order straight – self, sports, and then sex.

Padma – If you can't live with him, then live without him. In my Social Science class we had a big debate on interpersonal communication.

Tina – What's that?

Padma – Nothing really new, just a fancy way of analyzing your relationships with others. Like if someone gets on your nerves and says things that you don't like, then just tell them in a nice way. Don't hold it in. Say things like "When you say such and such or do such and such, it makes me feel such and such".

Tina – I have an aunt who says the same thing. She says that she is not going to hold things in. Let it out. She doesn't want an ulcer or a stroke. She says that it'll all come out in the wash.

Padma – Just don't forget to be nice about it. And don't text your breakup.

Store Theft

[Act I: Scene 5. Aretha and Mai Ling are seen sitting in a booth at the restaurant.]

Aretha – You'll never guess what happened to Cedric last Saturday.

Mai Ling – What happened? Did he get so high and pass out in church?

Aretha – No

Mai – Did he get locked out of his home and was homeless for the night?

Retha – No

Mai – Did he steal somebody's car and cause it to be totaled?

Aretha – No, but you're getting close.

Mai – Okay. I give. What happened to Ced?

Aretha – He got caught stealing from the Thrift Store.

Mai – What? A bakery?

Aretha – No, a thrift store sells used clothes and other merchandise. You're thinking about the thrift bakery that sells day-old bread and cakes. The thrift store gets clothes that people donate to the poor. They're used clothes; hand-me-downs. The store gets the clothes for free, washes them, and later sells them for a profit. They can get a coat for nothing and sell it for $20 or more.

Mai – Wow! People are always coming up with a hustle.

Aretha – Yeah, but what was so weird was that Ced got caught stealing from these people.

Mai – How did he do it? I bet it was easy. A store like that probably doesn't have a fancy security system.

Aretha – You're right. They don't have electronic sensors on their merchandise like fancy department stores. This is not Neiman-Marcus or Bloomingdales. This store doesn't even have a security guard. I mean, who would steal from a thrift shop? My mom told me that on some days they have a three-for-one dollar sale.

Mai – Get outta here. You mean you can get three items for just one dollar? That's incredible!

Aretha – Yeah, like on a Sunday, you can get three shirts or three pairs of slacks for just a dollar. You can get three sheets, pillow cases, whatever, for the same price the manager decides to put on sale. They have a color-coded system.

Mai – Color-coded. Why? What's that?

Aretha – They might say that all blue or red-tagged merchandise is three-for-a-dollar, while other merchandise coded yellow and green can be purchased at the regular price.

Mai – Yeah, but even the regular prices are low. You said that you can get a coat for just $20 or less.

Aretha – Yep!

Mai – So what did Ced steal and why and how?

Aretha – Cedric would put on the store's shirt over his shirt to see if it fit. Then he would take the shirt off and put it in his shopping cart. He would then put on another shirt. If it fit, he would place it also in the cart. If it didn't fit, he would hang it back on the rack. After about 15 or 20 minutes in the shirt aisle, he would look at pants and then shoes.

Mai – Did he put the pants on as well?

Aretha – No, he wouldn't. He just sized them up to see if they fit. The store doesn't have a fitting room to try on clothes. They have had too much stuff stolen in the past. He would then go to the jacket section and continue with the procedure. He would put on a jacket to see if it fit well. He would either place it in his shopping cart or return the item to the rack. He tried on jackets for another 15 or 20 minutes. Ced would then return to the shirt section and put shirts on and take them off.

Mai – Okay, I get the picture. But what did he steal and how?

Aretha – Well, Ced got caught when he went to the cashier to pay for the merchandise in his cart. The store manager had called the police, but Ced didn't know about it. As soon as Ced stepped outside after paying for his "new-used" clothes, a police officer questioned and searched Ced. Ced had on three shirts that he didn't pay for. They still had the store's tag on. When Ced was trying on jackets, he left his original jacket on the rack and exchanged it for one of the store's jackets. He did the same with a pair of shoes.

Mai – You mean to tell me that he walked out of the store without paying for a jacket, a pair of shoes, and three shirts. Man, that's unreal. Stealing from a used-clothes' place.

Aretha – What makes it so bad is that you can get many of the clothes real cheap, as I said, sometimes three-for-a-dollar. Nobody is that bad off or nobody should be that desperate.

Mai – He stole because he wanted to steal. He stole because he thought he was smart. Maybe he's a kleptomaniac.

Aretha – Yeah, maybe, but the store manager was smarter. He just let Ced steal, walk out of the store, only to be arrested by the police later.

Mai – Yep, you have to be careful when you think that you are slick and smart.

Aretha – Yep, cause some people are slicker and smarter.

Mai – I wonder. Is Cedric mentally challenged, as they call it now? Is he slow?

Aretha – Hey, I heard that he took Arielle to that lobster place for dinner one day. When it was time to pay the bill, he reached in his pocket and pulled out two coupons. He doesn't have a wallet, so when he was fumbling around with a bunch of loose papers and notes, a rubber pops out.

Mai – What' so unusual about that? Girls should be honored that a guy has a prophylactic in his pocket. That shows that he cares about his health and he is careful.

Aretha – Normally, that's so true, but in this case it was not an ordinary rubber.

Mai – What was it then, some generic brand from the dollar store? Oh, don't tell me that he stole it from the thrift store.

Aretha – No, worse. This was a *used* rubber.

Mai – Used?

Aretha – Yeah! He uses rubbers. He goes out on a date, washes them out, and then reuses them later.

Mai – That's nasty and unreal. I thought that you are supposed to use them once and throw them right away. I can see why he did it, but that doesn't make it right. Certain things shouldn't be reused.

Retha – He felt that if he washed it out, then it should be okay. As far as he was concerned, it shouldn't make a difference.

Mai – It makes a world of difference. I remember in my Chemistry class, the teacher was talking about reusing plastics and recycling bottles. There was something about the chemicals used to make plastic containers. You know, when people put food up for storage.

Retha – Yeah, leftovers.

Mai – Right! Well the teacher said that certain plastic containers should never be reused. In fact, water bottles should not be recycled. She said also that water bottles should not be exposed directly to sunlight because somehow chemicals in the plastic container can leak into the water. On some water bottles, there is an explicit warning about re-usage.

Retha – I don't know about that. Look at all those microwavable plastic containers that people use. People have been washing them out and reusing them for years.

Mai – Just because people do it doesn't make it right. What if harmful chemicals are leaking into your food while you are zapping your dinner in those radioactive contraptions called microwaves?

Aretha – You sound like my grandmother. One of her daughters gave her a microwave oven for Christmas and she gave it to someone else on their birthday. She said that she has been warming her food up the old-fashioned way for years, either on top of the stove or in the regular oven, and that was good enough for her.

Mai – That's what I'm talking about.

Retha – Yeah, but we're talking about reheating food for a minute or two. It's not like cooking a Thanksgiving turkey for hours at a time. I think that it is harmless, and so do millions of other people.

Mai – I see your point, but reusing rubbers may not be a good idea. What if germs from one girl remain undetected? It's like some invisible residue. Those microscopic germs can then be transmitted to another.

Retha – What is the likelihood of that occurring? One in a million! He probably had those rubbers in his pocket for a month. He's not a player. In fact, they may have been in his pocket for a year.

Mai – That's even worse. They could have been dry-rotted.

Retha – Well, I heard Arielle was very upset and put the word out and Ced couldn't get a date for months.

Mai – He couldn't get a date anyway, but this just made things worse. Sometimes he acts retarded, but he could just be really creative.

Retha – Well, in my opinion, stealing from a thrift store and reusing rubbers is not very creative.

Mai – Yeah, but I remember he had us cracking up at lunch one day. He told us how he acts during his IEP meetings.

Aretha – What's that?

Mai – IEP stands for Individualized Educational Plan for special needs' students. He said that he starts scratching his head, then he scratches under his arm, and then he goes back to scratching his head again.

Aretha – That's not smart. The psychologist might think he's got bugs. He might have fleas, lice, or bed bugs.

Mai – People don't have fleas; dogs and cats have them. And bed bugs are in the bed, not on people.

Aretha – That's not true. You can have a serious infestation of fleas in the house that first started with a dog or a cat. When there are so many of them, the fleas start attacking people.

Mai – Get outta here!

Aretha – Yes, it's true. The fleas start biting you around the ankles first and then up both of your legs, around the calf section or shin. My cousin had them. He had about a hundred red marks, resulting from flea bites, on each leg. He had to go to the doctor and get some ointment. The dog had to be washed every week. The house had to be sprayed with chemicals and fumigated once a month.

Mai – Wow, you learn something every day. But in this case, Ced was scratching like it was a nervous tick. He never scratched in class. This was just a ruse or an act for the interview with the social worker. He also started drooling.

Aretha – Like a baby with spit coming out of his mouth?

Mai – Yep, like a baby or a drunk. Check this out. This is the picture. He's got this saliva oozing down the sides of his mouth. It is gross. He must have eaten something prior to the interview in order to create this effect. Sometimes he wipes it off with his sleeve, while other times he lets it linger like a long strand of spaghetti dangling on one side of his cheek. It's disgusting to think about it.

Aretha – Why does he act so weird if he isn't?

Mai – He says that he gets more money. His mom gets $1500 a month and she gives him half for his performances.

Aretha – He gets money from the government for acting slow?

Mai – Yeah, that's why he thinks he's *so* smart when he acts *real* slow.

Aretha – That's messed up. So slow people are really smart? Well then I guess smart people are really slow. That is really illogical logic.

Mai – Well, not in the case of the store manager. He seemed slow to take action, but he was really smart.

Aretha – You're right!

Framed

[Act 2: Scene 1 – High school cafeteria at lunchtime. Seated at lunch table are Arthur and Berra who are best friends.]

Arthur – Billy got framed for hitting his girlfriend. He's been suspended and may face criminal charges. *[Arthur is just playing with his food while Berra is eating his like it's his last meal like a prisoner on Death Row.]*

Berra – Why do you say he got framed? Everybody knows that Bill is a bully. He pushes boys around. He's so unbearable. People have seen him push Becky around before. He likes to argue. He has a history of bullying. Why are you defending him?

Arthur – I'm defending him because I was there. I saw Becky argue and put her finger in his face and all he did was move her hand away and slapped her.

Berra – Ok, you saw him slap her. Guilty as sin!

Arthur – No he isn't. He slapped her and then she ran into the washroom. He went on to class... and so did I. Then, about fifteen minutes later, she went to the principal's office with two teeth knocked out and a swollen lip. He couldn't possibly have caused that amount of damage from just a slap in the face.

Berra – So what do you think happened? *[Arthur drinks his milk and eats his dessert.]*

Arthur – For some reason she wanted to crucify him. She must have gone into the restroom and busted her own lip and knocked out her own teeth.

Berra – Where do you get these crazy ideas? Hey – you want those fries?

Arthur – Naw.

[Bear reaches over and eats Artie's fries one at a time.]

Berra – What possessed Becky to dream this up?

Artie – Remember the sub Grandpa? You know, the substitute teacher that the kids affectionately called Gramps. He would tell us stories about the good ole days. I think he did it so we wouldn't act up.

Bear – Yeah, I remember Gramps. I remember when he got that name. Angie was a freshman; she was about fifteen. He came into the class and started to take attendance. The kids were being very rude and obnoxious. They were talking so loud that he couldn't be heard even after he started shouting at the top of lungs like he was at a football game. Talking nonsense about "If you youngsters don't settle down, everybody will be marked absent." He looked around. He looked lost and confused. He had a look on his face that said, "I don't know what to do next?" He looked like a goldfish in a shark tank. He was right, I mean, he could have marked everybody absent, but that would have been illogical. For instance, the twins never ditch classes, so if they were not accounted for, their moms would pitch a fit. Gramps would have lost his job.

Artie – Yeah, and he probably gets minimum wage.

Bear – Yep. So Gramps must have realized the no-win situation, swallowed his pride and changed his tune. Then Angie came up to him and said, "Would you like for me to take attendance for you. I know everybody." He replied, "Thank you very much young lady." Well she took attendance within a minute, effortlessly. He was amazed and said "Thanks again young lady, I mean Angela. Forgive me for staring at you but you remind me of my granddaughter. No offense." To this Angie replied, "No offense taken."

Artie – So ever since then we started calling him Gramps or Grandpa?

Bear – Yep. It caught on, especially by the bad boys in the class. They don't like calling any adults Mr. So and so or Mrs. So and so. They needle Mr. Watkins and Mr. Nicholson too death. Sometimes they call Mr. Watkins, Johnny or John, referring to his first name. They call Mr. Nicholson "old St. Nick" or just "Nick". It's so embarrassing. Kids today have no respect for authority or their elders. Well Gramps must have understood the teen psyche because he allowed the nickname to stick and the kids loved it. He didn't mind if they called him Gramps and everybody fell in love with him.

Artie – I think that they loved him for more reasons than that. He is so cool. He doesn't get upset like most teachers and parents. When we do something wrong, he usually gives you a look that says it all. I don't ever remember him ever raising his voice, except for that time when he said, "Class, I need your attention please" and later when he said "Everybody will be marked absent!" It seems like he immediately realized his mistake, calmed himself down, allowed Angie to take attendance, and kind of reinvented himself on the spot.

Bear – I don't get that phrase, people reinventing themselves. How can you reinvent yourself when you didn't invent yourself in the first place? It seems stupid.

Artie – Yeah, but it's like changing yourself or improving on yourself to be a better person. It's like on New Year's Eve when people make New Years' resolutions. They want to quit smoking or drinking or procrastinating. The biggest resolution is to exercise or lose weight. Now most of the time they fail to live up to their own expectations or aims or goals, but in reality they are trying to "reinvent" themselves.

Bear – Oh yeah, I see. Like women do a makeover or like that TV show that renovates a house.

Artie – Yeah, you got it.

Bear – Yeah, I see now. Gramps lost his cool once and then reinvented himself. Now he is usually cool, calm, and collected.

Artie – I remember one time some boys tried to set up Grandpa. Two boys got into a fight because they *wanted* Gramps to break it up. They were hoping that while Gramps was breaking up the fight, one of the boys would hit Gramps real hard, acting like they were trying to hit the other boy and seriously hurt Gramps. Their plan was to get Gramps to grab one or both of them while they were scuffling. After the fight or brawl was over, they would then later go to the washroom, bruise their own arms, and then go to the main office to complain. They planned to tell the principal and the nurse that Gramps had grabbed their arm, squeezed it and abused them. The problem or dilemma was if Gramps didn't grab on one of them, they would still be happy because one of them would have hit a teacher, possibly injuring him.

Bear – Wow, that's very devious. They could hit a teacher and not be charged because it looked like an accident. It looked like they were swinging on each other. Also, if Gramps grabbed their arms, they could charge corporeal punishment or something. These boys would have the entire class as witnesses. The principal would interview everybody in the room, the good kids and the bad, and everybody's story would correlate. He,

Gramps, would be crucified. He would be fired and then possibly criminally prosecuted. Gramps was in a no-win situation.

Artie – Well the plan backfired because Gramps never touched anyone. They tried to frame Gramps, but it didn't work. You see, Gramps told them to break it up, but he didn't lay a hand on them. So when these boys started playing around, Gramps walked up to them and started his speech. You know the one. It starts off with, "Now fellows, you don't want to be suspended. Let's break this up. Stop playing around. Let's settle down and move on." Well these boys knew the speech by heart. Their plan was to get Gramps physically involved. But Gramps didn't fall for it. He kept talking, in a relaxed, calm manner. He didn't get excited. It's like he had foreknowledge of their plan or he had some kind of spiritual intuition. When one boy started to bleed because the playing around got more intense, then the unbelievable happened.

Bear – What?

Artie – Well, when they kept tussling, two football players broke it up by separating the fighters. They did it because they just liked Gramps 'cause he was so cool and down to earth.

Bear – Wow! That is so cool.

Artie – Two of the biggest and baddest boys in the class pulled the two fighters apart.

Bear – So Gramps was in the clear.

Artie – Gramps never took his hands out of his pockets.

Bear – So how does this relate to Billy being framed?

Artie – Well after the scuffle, Gramps asked the boys if they wanted to report the incident or if they just wanted to shake hands and forget about it.

Bear – So what did they say?

Artie – Well the boy who came up with the original idea to frame Gramps said that he could forget about it. He knew that if he was sent to the principal's office he would be suspended or expelled. He has had so many prior convictions that nobody in the office liked him. The other boy, who just went along with the plan at first, said that he didn't want to report it, but since he was the one who actually got hurt and was bleeding, he had to do a double-take. First, he went into the coatroom and started punching the wall.

Bear – He was that mad? He's that strong? Is he crazy? Punching holes in the wall?

Artie – Yeah, you see the walls are made out of plasterboard so if you hit it just right, you can punch a hole in it. Well, he made a few holes in the wall. After he was in the coatroom for a minute, Gramps asked him if everything was all right.

Bear – How could everything be alright if he was punching holes in the closet?

Artie – I know. Gramps was just being cool and sarcastic. Well the boy said, "No, everything is not all right. I want to report the fight."

Bear – But if he reports the horsing around as a fight, then both of them might be suspended.

Artie – I know. That's why Gramps gave them an out. But this fellow was so embarrassed, he decided to report it. Both were interviewed and both were suspended. The boy who started the scuffle and came up with the idea of framing Gramps got a 5-day suspension and the loser who squealed got a 3-day suspension.

Bear – And what happened to Gramps?

Artie – He did nothing wrong. He tried to break it up but he didn't physically break them apart. See it's tricky for teachers. If they break up a fight and no one gets hurt, their jobs are safe. But if they break it up and in the process they mistakenly get hurt or one of the fighters gets injured, then the teacher might lose his job. That teacher might be out of work. Isn't that whack! I saw once in grammar school a teacher holding a bully's arms so that he could no longer hit a smaller kid and then the smaller kid stole on the bully. Also, if a teacher gets hurt breaking up a fight, the school may not pay his hospital bill.

Bear – Get out of here. If you do the wrong thing you get penalized; if you do the right thing, you get penalized.

Artie – Once I saw him thank Angie, but he didn't shake her hand, pat her on the head or back, or give her the high five. When people try to shake Gramps' hand, he balls his hand into a fist and gives them a friendly fist-to-fist punch.

Bear – Oh, like the power punch or victory punch the President gave his wife when they announced his victory.

Artie – Yep, but you know the President of the United States isn't the only one or the first one to come up with that type of recognition, but perhaps he made it more popular.

Bear – Yeah, I remember one time two girls were arguing. Gramps walked between them, talked to them calmly, and defused the situation without laying hands on them. Through the entire incident, he kept his hands in his pockets.

Artie – Right! That's what Gramps always does.

Artie – Well a teacher is in a precarious position. I remember another incident when two boys came out of one class; they were brothers who intended to jump this other guy coming out of his class. Well the two brothers started beating and stomping on the other guy. The little guy, who was alone, was being pummeled. Nobody tried to break it up. This was real drama! I remember the Gym teacher telling them to stop. They didn't respond. The Gym teacher immediately grabbed one of the brothers, the bigger of the two, and held him. You see, it was unfair; two against one. So while the teacher was holding on to the big brother, the little brother was still kicking the heck out of the other boy. The teacher needed help but couldn't walk away from the fight. Finally another teacher came. In fact, two other teachers came and separated the boys.

Bear – So what went wrong? I don't see what the problem was.

Artie – All of the boys' parents had to be notified. The mother of the two brothers said she was at work and couldn't take off right away. She said that if they started it, then they should be suspended. She just washed her hands off the incident. I think that she was just tired of them always getting into trouble. She knew that they were probably guilty. Come on now, two against one. But the other boy's mother, she came up to school right away, to complain.

Bear – What did she complain about? This is a public school. Anything and everything goes down here.

Artie – She complained to the principal about the teacher who broke up the fight. She was mad that her son had a black eye and a busted lip.

Bear – But you said that the teacher, the Gym teacher, grabbed the bigger of the two boys, and waited for assistance. What else could he have done?

Artie – Well, she was mad because he didn't stop the fight. She felt that he should have grabbed both boys who were the antagonists.

Bear – How could the Gym teacher grab both boys? One brother was as big as the teacher and the other is wiry and slippery.

Artie – I know. She was expecting the impossible. She was mad that her son got injured and she tried to have the teacher fired.

Bear – Some of these parents are unreasonable. I don't think that I would ever want to be a teacher or a principal.

Artie – Yep, some parents are crazy and some are stoned and high. Others are downright stupid.

Bear – Yep, that's why some kids are stupid. They get it from their parents.

Artie – My grandmother says that the apple doesn't fall too far from the tree.

Bear – That's really corny but accurate. Man, I don't think that I'll ever be a teacher. You try to help people out and you get screwed. The parents don't like you unless you give their little darlings good grades. The principal doesn't like you unless you laugh at his lame jokes. And now you tell me that students and parents set up and try to frame the teachers on a regular basis.

Artie – Well, the Gym teacher was cleared. He had to get a union steward to protect him and argue his case. It was decided that the Gym teacher did all he could do by restraining the bigger of the two boys. You know Nadia, right? She tried to get Mr. Lewis fired.

Bear – Another mock-fight?

Artie – No, she was really jealous that Mr. Lewis was giving so much attention to Claudia and none to her.

Bear – I can see why. Claudia is so fine. Man she looks like a super-model. And she has the nerve to wear those low-cut blouses with no bra. And what about those see-thru sun dresses? They are so sheer that when you catch her in the sun's rays, it's like looking at a butt-naked woman.

Artie – Well from what I heard and saw, Mr. Lewis gave Claudia a lot of attention but he never touched her. He would walk over to her, lean over her shoulder, and offer assistance. He never did anything unprofessional. Heck, you can't even tell these kids how to dress. They'll cuss you out and then their parents will try to get you fired. But the real deal was that Nadia was jealous. She wanted some attention.

Bear – Yeah, but Nadia looks like a Gremlin that was just run over by a Mack truck. I mean nobody in their right mind would give her any attention.

Artie – Well, she craves it all the same. She told her mom that Mr. Lewis was feeling on her breasts.

Bear – Impossible! Mr. Lewis never looked in her direction. When did this happen; after school or in her dream?

Artie – Both. She claimed that it happened after school but it really must have happened in her dreams. She said that at first she was grading papers for him after school and as she was handing him, that is Mr. Lewis, papers or he was handing her papers, his hand brushed against her blouse near her nipples. She said it happened more than once. According to her, since she didn't object and just ignored it, he then complimented her on her breast size and squeezed them.

Bear – No way! First of all, no one in their right mind wants Nadia. Second, Mr. Lewis can't be that stupid. Here she is seventeen and he is at least thirty or forty. If he were to touch anybody, it would be Claudia. I would give my right arm for a night in the sack with her; but Nadia, she makes me puke.

Artie – Well, Mr. Lewis was called into the principal's office the other day. In there were Nadia, her mother, the counselor, and the principal.

Bear- They were out to get him like a school of piranhas.

Artie – Maybe. Maybe not. They were out to get to the bottom of the matter. First, Nadia gave her interpretation of the story.

Bear – And what was Mr. Lewis' defense or reply?

Artie – He said that the alleged action was impossible.

Bear – Why, because Nadia is so ugly that nobody would touch her with a ten-foot pole.

Artie – No, he had to be professional. He said that it was impossible for him to molest Nadia in the classroom. Whenever he has students help him grade papers after school, he always makes sure that he has three or more kids present in the room. If he only has two students, he tells them that he has to leave early. Two kids are not enough. What if one of them has to go to the washroom? Then he would be alone with one student. His defense was that he never has less than three students in a room. He said that the principal could verify his story by interviewing students in his class that have served as graders. He gives them the answer sheet, they grade the papers, and then he pays them with a dollar or two. Sometimes he will buy chips and pop and pizza.

Bear – He doesn't pay much.

Artie – The kids don't need the money. I have seen Aretha in the room grading papers with the other students.

Bear – Aretha, that super-rich chick that drives a brand new Mercedes? They say her daddy is loaded. She lives up north with the rich folk. She definitely doesn't need a dollar.

Artie – I know. That's my point. Mr. Lewis gives everybody a dollar or a pop. If he has a lot of work that would take more than an hour, he orders pizza. The money is not the main issue. Kids help Mr. Lewis and grade his papers because they like him. He's cool and they get to socialize with each other in a relaxed environment.

Bear – Yeah, I've noticed that he doesn't always go around correcting people. Look at us, we're adults. We're grown. I'm eighteen. Some people in this school are twenty-one. We get tired of adults telling us what to do and correcting the way we talk and dress. Heck, some kids talk wrong just to get on the teacher's nerves. But Mr. Lewis is cool. You can even curse around him and he will either act like he doesn't hear it or will join in the conversation if it interests him.

Artie – Yeah, I remember once some boys were talking about their love lives. It got really heated. Then someone said something. I can't think of it now but maybe later it'll come to me. Well, this one boy was talking about something his girl did that was so stupid that all the boys in the group burst out laughing. Then Mr. Lewis interrupted and said, "That was funny, but I got a story, a real story that can top that." He then proceeded to talk about one of his ex-girlfriends who did some really stupid stuff. He couldn't have made it up that fast. This was undoubtedly a true story. Everybody busted out laughing. I laughed so hard, I cried. Peter had to walk around the room with his hands in the air because his side was hurting so much.

Bear – I see your point. Mr. Lewis has kids help him grade papers but they are really socializing and enjoying themselves.

Artie – Exactly! And that's why the money and the refreshments don't matter. Mr. Lewis told us that he has to give us something to protect him.

Bear – Protect him from what? How so?

Artie – He said that he doesn't want anybody to get the wrong idea that if they helped him, then he would be obligated to give them a better grade.

Bear – Yeah, like blackmail or something. I knew a lot of suck-ups in grammar school who did that.

Artie – Ms. Williams from our old grammar school called them sycophants.

Bear – What?

Artie – Sycophants! That's a fancy word for people who suck up to you because they want something in return.

Berra – Oh, like Mr. Barconi. He sucks up to anybody in authority. I have seen him kiss major butt. He sucks up to the principal, his assistant, the counselor, the psychologist, every parent and any big shot that comes to review the school.

Arthur – Yeah, I've seen him in action too. It's sickening. But maybe he does what he has to do. You know, jobs are hard to come by.

Berra – Yeah, but some people should be judged on their merit or their work performance.

Arthur – Just like us students. If we do the work then we should get the deserved grade. We shouldn't have to suck up to a teacher's every whim and idiosyncrasy.

Berra – Somebody needs to do a major overhaul of the public school system.

Arthur – Amen!

Berra – Yeah, and the way these teachers have to watch their backs all of the time. I imagine that's stressful.

Arthur – Yep, and when they are under stress, they put us up under stress.

Berra – Well, the bottom line is that we all have to watch our backs so we don't get framed - teachers, students, parents … everybody.

Arthur – And we have to watch our friends' backs too!

Anger Management

[Arthur and Berra are joined by Carmelita at the table.]

Arthur – On another note, did you hear about what happened in Music? Denzel went off on a teacher the other day. It was livid.

Berra – Denzel goes off on everybody. He has run-ins with students, teachers, principals, custodians, and even security. He shoved the principal in grammar school and got a 10-day suspension. Who did he pick on this time?

Artie – He went off on the Music teacher.

Bear – Ms. Taylor? She is so cool. Nobody should go off on her. She lets us listen to our own music. She doesn't judge us. Most teachers get bent out of shape when they hear cursing and lyrics that are not appropriate, but not her.

Carmelita – Yeah, I don't get it. Adults know that they curse too. They've heard the same songs on the radio. Some of the songs today are just renditions of oldies. I bet they don't turn a song off in their cars just because of a little cursing.

Bear – Yeah, and the music teacher is just a sub. Why did he want to go off on her? Like you said, she is so cool and laid back.

Artie – Well Denzel got mad because she played some classical music. I remember she called it the three top classics – the top B's – Beethoven, Brahms, and Bach.

Bear – I bet she got a big laugh when she said the top B's. You know what kids were thinking.

[Bear and Carmelita glance at each other, raise their eyebrows and smile.]

Artie– Yeah, there was a laugh. She probably said it on purpose to get their attention, knowing her. Well the CD only played for about a minute when Denzel shouted, "Hell no! We ain't having that crap up in here!" She tried to calm him down and explain that people need to be exposed to a variety of music. He then began cursing and saying, "I'll be a fool up in here! I'll be a fool up in here! We'll tear this mother up!"

Carmelita – Oh, you don't want to get him started. He really is a fool.

Bear – He's beyond foolish. He's dangerous.

Artie – I know. Well, he kept saying "I'll be a fool up in here! I'll be a fool up in here. We will tear this mother up." He then got four or five other people involved. They started chanting the same thing, in unison. Before you knew it, half the class was chanting, "I'll be a fool up in here. I'll be a fool up in here. We'll tear this mother up."

Bear – I see, it *was* getting serious.

Carmelita – And it sounded scary. It's no telling what they might do. They're about forty to fifty kids in that room.

Artie – Forty-six to be exact. And it was both scary and serious. Denzel threatened to overturn the piano.

Bear – Oh, he *is* nuts. That big piano that sits in the corner.

Artie – And then Bernard grabbed an electronic keyboard.

Carmelita – Those Yamaha piano keyboards that run on batteries? That thing is about three feet long!

Artie – Yep, and Sarah grabbed another keyboard also. They were getting ready to have a duel. You know, like swordfighters or fencing people. Sarah said, "On guard!" and Bernard said "Ready". They were about to swing when Ms. Taylor hollered, "Stop! I'm calling security!" They immediately stopped but then Bridget took the CD out of the cassette player, the one that was playing the classical music, and walked around the room saying, "Who wants to buy this fabulous classic. Let's start the bidding." Someone said, "I'll give you a penny." Someone else said "You should have started with a six-pence. That crap is not worth a penny." Everybody fell out laughing. It was hilarious. Ms. Taylor was running around the room like a chicken with her head cut off. She was trying to put our fires left and right. She needed her CD. She wanted the kids to stop horsing around. As soon as she would stop one or two kids from doing some mischief, someone else would get started.

Bear – All this was instigated by our beloved Denzel.

Artie – Exactly!

Carmelita – He is infectious.

Artie – Yep. Ms. Taylor wanted to get security, but our intercom system doesn't work. She couldn't leave the room to get help because there was no telling what would go down. If she left the room, she could get fired for leaving us kids unattended.

Carmelita – Yeah, people would start throwing things.

Artie – Or dissing people. When Denzel kept saying, "I'll be a fool up in here" other people joined in. If security didn't come in, these kids would be throwing books, pencils, and paper, anything they could get their hands on. One boy picked up a computer monitor. He acted like he was going to throw it at someone.

Bear – Unreal. You know how heavy and expensive those things are? They weigh at least 30 pounds and cost a couple of hundred dollars.

Artie – Yeah, these kids are crazy. They're loco. As soon as Ms. Taylor got him to settle down and give up the computer, someone else acted up.

Carmelita – You could get serious consequences for that action. That's destroying school property! Someone could be permanently maimed. The principal would have to notify your parents and the police.

Artie – Well, all of this started because Denzel didn't like the music selection. I mean, nobody really liked it, but he made his feelings public.

Bear – That's sad because you were in a music class. You're supposed to learn and be exposed to varieties of music.

Carmelita – But some people are so closed-minded. If it isn't their type of favorite music, they automatically hate it. People should open up their minds to diversity.

Artie – I agree. They also shouldn't be so sensitive. Denzel is dangerous. Who would have thought that a musical selection would trigger a riot?

Bear – I used to go to anger management classes at my other school. They said that people have so many issues, hate, and problems in their lives that the least little thing can set them off.

Carmelita – But how would the teacher know this. She is just a sub. She's not aware of Denzel's mental state. I heard that he was BD.

Bear –Not referring to being a gangbanger, I presume.

Carmelita – No. BD stands for behavior disorder. He has an IEP that documents his behavior and recommends learning strategies. He has been BD since kindergarten.

Bear – What is an IEP?

Carmelita – IEP is some term that the school counselor uses for Individualized Educational Plan. The kids that we call "slow" have to have one.

Bear – Many of those kids are not really slow; they're just pretending.

Carmen – Some are real, like Denzel. I was in a room once when one of the boys took a stapler and started shooting staples at people.

Bear – One of those loose staples could hurt you.

Carmen – Worse. More than just hurt. One hit in the wrong place could permanently maim you. You see, this was not an ordinary stapling gun. This was a heavy-duty gun that could be used to affix carpeting to a wooden floor.

Bear – That's insane! What's an apparatus such as that be doing in a classroom? Either the students are crazy or the teachers are.

Carmen – Maybe a little of both.

Bear – Yeah, well the teacher called security and the boy got a three-day suspension for shooting staples at other students and the teacher.

Carmen – He shot staples at the teacher? No way!

Bear – Yep. First he was playing around, shooting staples at his friends. They ducked and laughed. When the teacher confronted him and demanded the release of the gun, that is the stapling gun, he then shot staples at the teacher.

Artie – These kids have no respect for anybody!

Bear – You're right. So the teacher called school security, who then in turn called the police officer assigned to our school. The boy was arrested and handcuffed right there in class.

Artie – Man, it's sad that we have to have a police officer in the school to enforce discipline.

Bear – Well, we must be a good school because some schools have six to eight regularly assigned police officers. They have the same cops on duty all day every day, from 8 in the morning to 3 in the afternoon.

Carmen – Wow! That's unreal! They don't even have that many assigned to banks. I mean they have special security officers, usually just one in a small branch, with a gun and a walkie-talkie. If something is going down, the Robocop can call the real police. Now you're telling me that some schools have up to eight regular po-po in the school every single day. That's sad.

Artie – Yeah, that is sad and tragic. It's a sad commentary on our society. We need to get back to the days when students respected their teachers.

Carmen – And parents respected them.

Why Fight?

[Arthur, Berra, and Carmelita are now joined by Robert and Tina at the lunchroom table.]

Arthur – Why do boys fight all the time?

Robert – Girls like to fight too.

Artie – But why? What are they trying to prove?

Rob – You have to prove that you're no punk. You have to stand up for yourself. You can't let people push you around. My dad told me that if someone is messing with me, then I should stand up for myself. It doesn't matter if I am in school or around the house.

Artie – But if you fight in school, you're going to get suspended. You know that crack-head principal doesn't care who is right and who is wrong. She will suspend both parties and ask questions later.

Rob – I do what my pops tell me to do. I have to live with him. If he tells me to stand up for myself, then that's what I'm going to do, in school or out of school.

Artie – Yeah, but the more you fight, the more fights will be. What I'm saying is that first there is fighting, then stabbing, and later the ultimate, which is shooting someone. When is this violent cycle going to end?

Rob – Violence has been around since caveman days. The Romans had one of the best armies in recorded history.

America's armed forces were so bad once that in World War II other countries begged for our help. We didn't get involved in the world war until the Japanese bombed our Pearl Harbor in Hawaii.

Artie – I remember Mr. Sims talking about that in History. He said that Hitler wanted to rule the world and that he just used the Japanese emperor, pretending to be friends because he, Hitler and his German army, were fighting on two fronts, the Western and the Eastern, and he didn't have the resources to fight the Americans.

Rob – What were these two fronts, the Eastern and the Western?

Artie – Well one faced west and one faced east. I forgot which was which. But on one front the Germans were fighting the Russians and on the other front they were fighting the French and the English. They kind of worn their resources very thin. It got worse when the Americans decided to help the Russian, the English, and the French people.

Rob – I bet. So you're saying that Hitler had to be friends or pretend to be friends with the Japanese to achieve his goals.

Artie – Yeah, there was also some guy called Mussolini, from Italy, and somebody else in Russia. It might have been Stalin. Well at first, Hitler was friends with Stalin, then Hitler turned on Stalin, like a Doberman pinscher. Hitler was like the leader of a gang so he used other people to help him achieve his goal of world domination.

Robert – Well that's what I'm saying. Just as America had to prove that we were no punks, we had to go to war. Hitler invaded Poland and Czechoslovakia and they just punked out. He invaded their territory so fast that they didn't have time to respond. Hitler then invaded Russia and England also, but they kept fighting to the bitter end. Eventually, America came to their aid, but they had to fight for years all by themselves.

Artie – Like Mr. Sims said, the Allies, which included England, Russia, America, and some other countries, were the good gang warding off the evil attempts of the bad gang which included Germany, Italy, and Japan.

Rob – What was the bad gang called?

Artie – I forgot. It might have been something pertaining to a satellite or an axis.

Rob – Ok, that's what I'm saying homey. You have to fight for your rights and for your freedom and dignity and make sure your boys have your back. People will push you around if you let them. You have to stand up for your rights, for your freedom, and for your dignity.

Artie – Yeah, I remember Mr. Sims saying that the countries in Europe begged for America to intervene during the early stages of the war, but the American people kept saying no. I think the term was laissez-faire which means leave me alone because I don't want to get involved. The president at the time, the President of the United States, I think was Roosevelt. I forgot his first name but they called him FDR. He told the American people that Hitler would not stop at Poland and Czechoslovakia; that Hitler would try to run over all of Europe and eventually try to conquer the whole world.

Rob – And how did the American people react to their President?

Artie – They basically said that Europe's problem was Europe's problem. We don't want to get involved.

Rob – I can see their point. It's the same thing that's happening in my neighborhood. People don't want to get involved. If you join a fight then you have to continue to fight. Eventually someone is going to get hurt or killed. Why can't people just be civilized?

Artie – People don't want to be civil. They want to bully and be arrogant. They want to take what's yours and make it theirs.

Rob – I see your point. Hitler wanted to take over Poland and Czechoslovakia and make those people work for nothing. He wanted them to build tanks and airplanes and treat them as slaves. He even tricked the Jewish people into fake job offers. Mr. Simms said that jobs were hard to find in their recession, so Hitler spread a rumor that there were jobs in other places. The Jews then boarded certain trains that would take them to a new area where jobs would be plentiful. I think that is where they put entire families into railroad box cars that took them to the concentration camps.

Artie – Yeah, and at those camps, well that was just a staging area, until they went into the gas chambers.

Rob – Yeah, I remember the photographs when we had that cultural awareness display in the halls. I think millions of Jews were killed. But that's my point exactly. If you don't stand up for something, then you stand for nothing. If you don't fight, then evil people will take over your life and punk you out for the rest of your life. I would rather die fighting than let someone just steamroll over me.

Artie – But that's my point! Why do boys, and girls, have to fight. I know what you're saying, but it needs to come to a halt. All this violence – in school, at home, around the community – needs to cease. I want to live my life, focus on my dreams and goals, and not always look over my shoulder for a potential threat. How can we focus on college and our life-goals, when we are constantly focusing on fighting?

Robert – Dude, you have to do that thing called multi-tasking. You have to concentrate on more than one thing at a time to succeed in life.

Arthur – Yeah, I've heard of that before. It's like a juggling act in the circus.

Rob – Yep, but it's no joke. This is no clown act. You have to manage separate items in your life and bring them all to perfection. Success in life doesn't come cheap. You have to pay the piper.

Artie – What does that mean? Pay the piper.

Rob – I'm not totally sure. My grandmother has these old sayings that she just blurts out all the time. I think you have to pay the man who is playing the flute when he plays your favorite tunes. It's like a song request.

Artie – Oh, I see. So to be successful in life, you have to pay your dues.

Rob – That's another good analogy.

Artie – But that's not always true. There are some singers and actors who never paid their dues. They were discovered early. They were simply at the right place at the right time.

Robert – I guess everything is relative. What might work for one person may not work for another. You can't judge people by the actions of a few. Every situation is different and unique.

Arthur – So true. I still don't know why guys like to fight all the time.

[Carmen is slurping on a Slurpee and Tina is smacking on some chewing gum.]

Rob – There must be a better way to live.

Carmen – Yeah, but people say things to annoy or antagonize others on purpose. Just the other day Mary called Cindy's momma a whore!

Tina – But she is a hoe! Everybody sees her on the street from 6pm to 6am trying to cop a trick.

Carmelita – Ah, people say that but I don't think anybody has really ever seen her. That's all about hype. One person starts a rumor and then everybody else agrees with it for fear of being an outcast.

Tina – Nope, this is real. I personally saw her at the truck stop one morning.

Carmelita – That's no proof. A lot of people go there for breakfast. Some people say you get the best breakfast at places where truckers and police officers frequent.

Tina – But she wasn't eating breakfast. She was walking from truck to truck, talking to the drivers in the parking lot. Then I saw her jump in one cab.

Carmen – Ok, so she hitched a ride, but that's not enough proof.

Tina – Well, what about my uncle. He was drinking and playing cards with my dad and his friends one afternoon. I came home and they were sitting at the dining room table. I was about to go into my room when my dad told me to bring some beers from the fridge. While I was in the kitchen, I heard my uncle talking about this chick who was real cheap and would do anything and everything for a few dollars. He described her. He identified Cindy's mom to a tee. The police could use my uncle as a sketch artist to catch criminals because he has an eye for detail. I know from what he said that he tapped Cindy's mom. When I brought in the beers, everybody changed the subject. They started talking about the ball game as if they were talking about it previously. I wasn't embarrassed because I just played it off like I didn't hear anything before.

Carmen – Ok, I see your point but even if it's true, it is still wrong and impolite to talk about people behind their backs. What I'm saying is if you can't say something nice, then don't say anything at all.

Tina – My nana says that same phrase.

Carmen – I'm sure grandmothers around the world feel the same. We could avoid more fights and conflicts if we would just put harnesses on our mouths.

Tina – Harnesses?

Carmen – Yeah, like they put bits on horses. They put muzzles on vicious dogs to keep their mouths shut so they don't bite people. If people would restrain themselves before saying negative things about people, talking about them behind their backs, there would be less violence in the world.

Tina – Yeah, I saw Cindy go into the nurse's office. Her face was all messed up. She might have had two black eyes, missing teeth, and a scarred up face.

Carmen – That's what I'm talking about. If people kept their mouths shut, all of that might not have happened. I heard that Cindy was fighting two girls at once. She was just defending her mom's rep and she got jacked. The good guy doesn't always win in real life.

Tina – Somebody put the info on Facebook.

Carmen – That's what I'm saying. There is too much negative gossip going around. Why can't we have positive gossip, positive vibes, and uplifting energy emanating from our minds to enrich and refresh other people?

Tina – Wow! You must be some sort of philosopher or something.

Carmelita – I'm just a concerned kid who thinks for herself.

Cell Phones

[Act II: Scene 2. Carlos and Ernesto are seated at another table in the lunchroom.]

Carlos – Did you hear about Vicki?

Ernesto – Yeah, I heard she got hit by a drunk driver and she's in intensive care at the hospital.

Carlos – Well you got half of it right. She's in intensive care at St. Mark's, but the accident was her fault and the driver wasn't drunk.

Ernesto – What happened?

Carlos – She was running for the bus, talking on the phone, and ran into the street when a car changed lanes. The driver didn't anticipate her running across the street, jaywalking, against the light, in the midst of heavy traffic. I mean, what was she thinking?

Ernie – She was thinking about catching the bus.

Carl – Well, she should have thought better. It's so sad now because now she can't run, walk, talk, eat, or anything. They have her strapped to some machine and tubes are feeding her.

Ernie – Oh no! And all this because she was running to catch a bus.

Carl – Yep! This happened mainly because she was so engrossed in her conversation. They say cell phones cause so many accidents. You already know that it is illegal to drive and talk on the phone?

Ernie – I think everybody knows that but half of the time they don't enforce it.

Carl – You're right, but it's still dangerous. They say people get distracted and so wrapped up in their conversation that they aren't paying attention to all the situations that are evolving on the road.

Ernie – Yeah, but I can talk and drive. What if you're in the passenger's seat? I can talk to you and drive. I'm not easily distracted. I bet I won't get a ticket for talking.

Carl – That's true, but I read that driving and talking on a cell phone is a whole lot different. You can't compare apples to oranges. I read an article that said talking on a cell phone and driving increases your stress level by 5,000%.

Ernie – What?

Carl – They say that driving itself increases your stress level by 1,000% because you have to be aware of so many situations. You have to look at the cars in front of you, look at the traffic behind you, use your peripheral vision to check out what's on both sides, anticipate people walking, running, and kids on bikes, objects falling out of the sky ….

Ernie – Come on, you're exaggerating.

Carl – Not really. My dad says that insurance is so high for teenagers, in fact it is high for males under 35 because they don't pay attention to all of the possible driving scenarios. So driving alone increases your stress level by 1,000% and talking on a cell phone increases it by 5,000%.

Ernie – Ah, come on. You can't believe everything you see and hear. You can't believe everything you read.

Carl – That's true, but then why is the accident rate higher because people are talking on cell phones? They have scientists and statisticians who study this for a living. In some cities they were contemplating giving people a ticket for just walking and talking on a cell phone.

Ernie – Now that is absurd! You are really pulling my leg.

Carl – I'm not. Check it out. People walking in the congested metropolitan areas in our country, mainly the downtown cities, can get a ticket for merely walking and talking. They're walking and talking on their cell phones, totally oblivious to their surroundings. They have *documented cases* where people have been hit by cars, especially cabs, because they were talking on their cell phones, not paying attention to their surroundings.

Ernie – Ok, I see your point. I know for a fact how frantic some cab drivers are. I mean they zip in and out, do illegal things, all for a ride or a tip.

Carl – Maybe yes, maybe no. I don't believe that cabbies do illegal driving. Think about it. They get paid to drive. They are probably the safest, most responsible, drivers out there.

Ernie – Ok. I see your point.

Carl – There was one lady who walked against the light into a busy street downtown. The light didn't just turn red. It was red for at least thirty seconds. Everybody else was standing by the curb on the sidewalk. She was *so* into her conversation that she didn't notice anything. She didn't notice the people standing and waiting for the light to change. She didn't notice the cars flowing with the traffic. She didn't even hear the horns blowing. And then, "Wham!" She got struck down. Everybody was just befuddled. They couldn't believe it. That's why some cities want to give people tickets for walking and talking.

Ernie – I heard that some cities give you a ticket just for jaywalking.

Carl – What's that?

Ernie – Jaywalking is what she basically did. It's walking when the stoplight blinks "Don't Walk". It's crossing in the middle of the block, or really anywhere other than the corner.

Carl – I wonder why it's called "jaywalking".

Ernie – I think they got it from watching pigeons walk. They walk kind of crooked … zigzagging down the street.

Carl – Yeah, pedestrians can cause serious accidents to themselves and others.

Ernie – But some people think that the pedestrian *always* has the right of way.

Carl – Not true. Not true. We need to discuss this in class one day because so many kids would benefit. I know for a fact that many kids think that they always have the right of way. Check out dismissal time. See how ignorant they act. They walk right out into the street in droves, looking like a swarm of locusts on a wheat field.

Ernie – You are so dramatic.

Carl – Well check them out. Observe. You'll see how ridiculous and dangerous it is.

[Enter Rachel and Padma. Both girls sit down at the table.]

Rachel and Padma – [in unison] Hey, what's up?

Carlos – We were just rapping about the dangers of cell phones and what a nuisance they can be.

Rachel – Cell phones *are* a nuisance. I think that I'm going to get rid of mine.

Padma – Are you nuts? How are you going to exist without communicating to people?

Rachel – Well the problem is that people are *always* calling me and expecting me to stop what I'm doing to chat. I go to the library every day to play on the computers and I usually get twenty to thirty calls during the brief time I am in the library. The library has a two-hour computer limit and a no-talking cell phone policy. I go to the health club every day and I can't talk and work out at the same time. When I'm driving my mom's car, it's against the law to talk and drive. When I go to church, the bank, the currency exchange, and other places of business, it is considered impolite to talk on your cell phone.

Paddy – I understand all that, but this seems like an extreme measure to take. By trying to eliminate one problem, you are going to create more. You sound like the federal government.

Rachel – Well, our government does some weird things. Some people say that because of the health care bill, people without insurance will benefit, but the rest of the country will suffer with higher taxes. Thus eliminating one problem can cause more problems.

Paddy – Maybe. Maybe not. But what if the government eliminated fat from other programs, you know, start having cutbacks and stop paying people for duplicate services, then money would be saved that could go into the health insurance program. My uncle told me that when he goes to City Hall, he has to get in one line for one thing, another line for something else that is directly related to the first thing, and then still another line for a similarly related service. He said common sense would dictate that the first person be trained to complete all three transactions at their computer station. Instead of paying for three people to do one job, they could save money by only paying one person.

Rachel – That makes sense.

Paddy – Yeah. He has been around. He told me of the time when they had five garbage men on every truck to pick up trash in the neighborhood.

Rachel – Five people? I have only seen two; the driver and the dumper.

Paddy – Well, way back in the day, they had a driver, two dumpers, one person with a push broom who would sweep the alley, and a supervisor who would watch the crew.

Rachel – I see your point. I bet one day some cities will have only one person – the driver – who drives the truck and dumps the cans all by himself.

Padma – That day is here already. In my Social Science class, the teacher said that in some suburbs one person *does* drive the truck and pick up the garbage using some type of mechanical robotic arm.

Rachel – See, I'm a visionary. I can see into the future.

Padma – Ok. I'll give you your props this time.

Rachel – Thanks. If the government would cut back on employees then more money would be available for necessary programs.

Paddy – Yeah, but the solution to one problem might create more problems. Now you would have more people out of work who might then get on welfare or use unemployment insurance, costing the government more money.

Rachel – Life can get complicated. Perhaps I should just keep my phone and get a better reduced plan. I'm going to look into one of those pay-as-you-go monthly plans.

Paddy – That sounds more feasible. You might need a phone for emergencies. You might have to call 911 for someone. Somebody might be trying to beat you up or even kill you and you could call someone using the speaker phone feature so they could record the situation. Don't be penny wise and pound foolish.

Rachel – What in the earth does that mean?

Paddy – My grandfather said that some people work hard at budgeting every penny, clipping coupons and things and then waste money on big things. A pound in England is worth about a dollar. So some people spend a lot of time watching how they spend their pennies and waste big bucks at the same time.

Rachel – It must be great having your grandfather around to talk to and get wisdom. I never knew mine.

Padma – No problem. Come visit me. My gramps will unofficially adopt you. All you have to do is call him gramps and he will share his wisdom with you.

Rachel – That's a date!

[The girls leave the table.]

Cell Phones are a Nuisance

Carlos – I am so depressed. This cell phone is a trip. I don't know how I'm going to pay my cell phone bill. It quadrupled last month because I fell in love with Aretha and now she left me because she said I didn't answer the phone every time she called.

Ernesto – You're depressed because you can't pay your cell phone bill? Man, talk to your provider. Tell them you will pay half. Tell them you need a better plan, one with unlimited minutes. What are your minute's usage allotments per month?

Carlos – My plan is 450 minutes per month for $45. My bill was over $200. I was talking to Retha three or more times a day. She would call me and half of the time her messages went to voice mail. Man, does she leave long voice mail messages! And if I didn't call her back within the hour, she would send extended text messages. That's what really ran my bill up. She can write a book texting. I would get a text message from her, and there would be eight or more segments to the message.

Ernesto – Well some chicks are longwinded. Some feel more comfortable texting on the phone instead of having a real conversation. I think they feel as though they are insulated.

Carl – Insulated from what?

Ernie – They feel that they can say anything without immediate repercussions. It's like if they say something stupid or hurtful, you can't get mad and hit them upside the head. Your only response is to text them back or ignore. It sounds like all you need is an unlimited calling plan. You could probably get one for about $60 a month. That's a lot cheaper than $200. You could get unlimited text too.

Carl – Yeah, I know. I got online and did some research. Why do I now need unlimited talk and text if I have no one to communicate with? I'm not really depressed. You see, I'm kind of happy that we broke up.

Ernie – Think positive. Get it now for the future. You will meet someone else. You're young. Did you ever suspect that you were going over your limit?

Carl – Nope. I would call her before 8 in the morning and would usually talk at length, and then later after 9 o'clock at night I would call her again. I thought I was doing the right thing. When I got the bill, I almost had a heart attack. It said that the hours from 6 – 8 a.m. were peak coverage, and all of her voicemail and text messages must have caused my bill to skyrocket.

Ernie – Well the past is past. Don't cry over spilled milk. Learn from your mistakes and move on. Pay half of the bill now, get a new plan, look for a new girl, and move on with your life.

Carl – That's easy for you to say. Aretha said that she left me because of a cell phone. She said that every time she called, I never picked up the phone. That's bull-crap. I admit that half of the time I didn't pick up, but that's because I was busy or couldn't afford to pick up the phone. She lives on the other side of town with the rich folks. I was just kidding myself that things would work out, but you know (*pause*) … opposites attract.

Ernie – So was she equally attracted to you as well or was this a one-sided love affair?

Carl – Man, she loved my dirty drawers. I did things to her that I won't confess up to. I made her shiver and quiver. I even told her that I would make her beg and whimper.

Ernie – You told her to her face that she would beg for it? Man, are you arrogant or crazy?

Carl – Perhaps it is a bit of both. You can call it arrogance; I would just call it damn good. I have confidence in myself.

Ernie – Something's not right here. If you are so darn good and she is so rich, why didn't she just pay your phone bill? Why didn't she just give you a phone with unlimited calling to keep up with you? When women call men ten times a day, they are really checking up on their man. They don't want other women messing with their stuff.

Carl – Yeah, but even if I had an unlimited plan, I don't think I would want to talk all day. I would be in a class and get text messages. When Aretha asked me why I didn't text her back, I couldn't give her a satisfactory answer. Kids text each other in class all the time. The teachers know about it, but as long as you're quiet, it's no big deal. I didn't text her back because I was either focusing on the lesson or worried how I would pay the phone bill. Either way she was unhappy.

Ernie – You reminded me of one day in Biology and everybody was texting each other the answers to the test and Mr. Jackson never once got up from his seat. We had a ball! But something about your situation doesn't mesh here. If you could make her quiver and shiver, why would she leave you for something as simple as not talking on the phone?

Carl – Yeah, I thought about that. I kept going over and over in my mind what went wrong. I started replaying every scene of our time together. Everything seemed so perfect.

Ernie – Well, something wasn't right. I can't see a girl leaving something that is so good just because you didn't answer the phone. She must have had another dude on the side.

Carl – That's possible but I don't want to acknowledge it. In fact, anything is possible. She could have had a chick on the side. I don't really think so, but it's possible. There *was* something she said that did stick out in my mind when she broke off with me.

Ernie – What did she say?

Carl – She called me and said, "I can't do this anymore." Then she went on and on with this tirade about me not picking up the phone every time she called. But what shook me up was the phrase, "I can't do *this* anymore."

Ernie – Why did that shake you up so?

Carl – It sounded like she was in an acting class. Like she was putting on a façade or a charade and she was now tired of playing her role. She reminded me of those old movie stars like Bette Davis or Marilyn Monroe.

Ernie – Where are you going with this? Why are you bringing up ancient history about old movie legends?

Carl – That phrase reverberated in my soul. She said, "I can't do this anymore." I kept asking myself what is *this*? Then it dawned on me what *this* was.

Ernie – Well please divulge this information before I fall off the edge of my seat. The suspense is killing me. What was *this*?

Carl – Her reference to *this* is related to those ancient movie stars. You see, she was just playing a game. She accused me of playing games, such as answering the phone when it was convenient only for me, but in reality she was the real player. I put all my cards on the table face up. I told her that I would make her beg for it. I told her that my only goal was to make her happy. That happiness was based on fulfilling her sexual, emotional, mental, and spiritual needs. I was up front. I had no hidden agendas. But here is the real deal. She was just pretending to love me, to see what a dude from the other side of the tracks could do. I was like an experimental rat in the Science lab.

Ernie – So when she said, "I can't do this anymore" she was really referring to her acting abilities?

Carl – Right on. Exactly! She couldn't keep up the charade. Or maybe she just got bored with her own acting. All of her whimpering, quivering, and begging for more was just a ruse to play me.

Ernie – But what do you have that she needs? If she really didn't want the sex, or your company, or your conversation, what could you possibly have to add to the relationship? She's rich and you're poor. You have no money, no prospects of getting any money, and she really doesn't need anything because her daddy spoils her rotten.

Carl – That's where you are 90% right and 10% wrong. I have nothing and she seemingly has everything. But as I was reviewing our time together, she always implied that she needed things, or should I say, she wanted things. She needed nothing. Her daddy makes sure that she wants for nothing. This girl has over three hundred pairs of shoes, hundreds of purses, dozens of watches, etc. She is the ultimate material mama. But what she really wanted was a chump to buy her more things. I can feel it now.

Ernie – Wait a minute. She has everything and still wants more.

Carl – Yep, like a compulsive gambler, alcoholic, or shopaholic. My grandfather has a phrase about people like that. He would say, "They have two loaves of bread under each arm and they are still standing in the bread line."

Ernie – That's funny. Where did he come up with that phrase?

Carl – He said that during the 1930s people were out of work because of the Great Depression.

Ernie – I heard that mentioned before. I think I heard in a history class. What was that?

Carl – The Great Depression was like an economic recession when thousands, no millions of people, were out of work. There were no jobs available. Businesses folded. In fact, most of the banks closed because they had no money. People who *had* money in the bank and in the stock market lost everything. Can you imagine having, let's say, a hundred thousand dollars in the bank and you go up to the teller and say that you would like twenty thousand of your money, and the teller tells you, "No"?

Ernie – How can the teller do that? It's your money. They have to give it to you if you ask for it.

Carl – How can they give it to you if they don't have it? See the banks don't always keep your money in the vault. They take your money and invest it in the stock market. That's why they pay you interest on your own money. Let's say you put $1,000 in the bank and they pay you 5% interest. You get an extra fifty dollars at the end of the year. But what they do is invest *your* money. They invest the $1,000 in the stock market and might make 30% interest off it. This is how the bankers make money. They made 30% by investing your money and give you back a measly 5%, thus resulting in a 25% profit off of your own money.

Ernie – That should be illegal.

Carl – No it isn't. You can invest your own money in the stock market, but you would have to conduct a lot of research and stay abreast of new technologies. So during the Depression, banks folded and went out of business because of bad investments. They invested people's monies and things didn't work out. As a result of so much unemployment and poverty in America, the government and local churches gave out free bread, soup, and other items to people so that there would not be riots and chaos in the streets. All the people had to do was stand in long lines and wait their turn. That's where my gramps got the phrase of standing in line with a loaf of bread under each arm and still expecting a handout.

Ernie – We still have remnants of that today. I've seen people stand in line at churches on Saturday mornings and receive one or two bags of groceries.

Carl – Yeah, that's because some people say that we are in a recession, but a depression is hundred times worse. Some people say that people today are just lazy and are just looking for a handout and don't really want to work.

Ernie – So you're saying Aretha is just greedy. She wanted you to buy her things but she really needed nothing.

Carl – Exactly! Perhaps she's just a gold-digger.

Ernesto – Well if she is, she will just end up with a bucket full of mud and no gold messing with your sorry-ass.

Carlos – Very funny, but so true.

Ernie – Well it's good that you found out early before your phone bill was $1,000 a month or you started working two jobs to pay for her shopaholic compulsive behavior.

Carl – Thanks man. You're a true friend. By venting with you, I was able to sort things out and get things into perspective.

Ernie – Hey, that's what friends do. I'm there for you, always.

PROSTITUTION

[Act II: Scene 3. Aretha and Mai Ling are sitting at another lunchroom table in the school.]

Aretha – I was walking to the store and some guy tooted at me.

Mai – Tooted?

Aretha – Yeah. He was in a black shiny car. He tooted his horn, slowed down and stopped the car. He lowered the passenger side window and whispered, "Hey pretty girl, you want $10?" I looked at him like he was a fool and kept walking. Then he eased up in his car and said "Ok, no problem. I got $20."

Mai – What did you do then?

Aretha – I said "$20 for what?" He then said, "Whatever you feel comfortable with"

Mai – What did you do then?

Aretha – I walked away fast. I started looking around for some elderly lady or a minister or somebody.

Mai – Why did he seek you out?

Aretha – Damned if I know! Maybe he liked my legs in my 'Daisy Dukes'.

Mai – What are 'Daisy Dukes'?

Aretha – They're real short short-shorts. I mean you can even see some booty cheeks.

Mai – You were walking down the street with them nasty things on? Those are like booty-shorts. Naw, he didn't merely like your legs, he was checking out your whole body. What else did you have on, if anything?

Aretha – I had on a low cut top, but everybody wears them in school. It's no big deal. In fact the boys in school don't even look 'cause everybody's wearing them. Hey, I was minding my own business.

Mai – Slit no. You were trying to drum up some business and when opportunity knocked, you punked out.

Aretha – Shut up! I can wear what I want when I want. This is America. This is a free country. I am free to express myself through my fashions.

Mai – Yeah, it's free all right if you give it up for free. All I'm saying is that you advertised and you found a mark and got scared.

Aretha – What's a mark?

Mai – A mark is like a chump, somebody you can run a con game on. A patsy, a punk, a fool, a trick or a dupe.

Aretha – Ok. Ok. I get the message.

Mai – Well then, you advertised your merchandise like a fisherman puts a worm on a fishhook. You dangled your booty in the waters and got a nibble. The only reason he didn't bite was because you swam away.

Aretha – Well I wasn't planning on it and I'm not a two-bit whore.

Mai – You say that but your clothes said something differently. Have you heard the phrase "Dress for Success"? Well you dressed for "Suck-it".

Aretha – Stop! Stop it! Rock stars, pop stars, and fashion models, everybody, just about everybody, dresses provocatively.

Mai – Not everybody. You're lucky it wasn't a snatch and grab.

Aretha – Yeah, well like I said most of the boys at school don't even look. I *make* some of them pay attention, like Derrick. I always manage to drop my pen or pencil when I'm near him so I can bend over or squat down so he can get a better look.

Mai – What about Mr. Williams, the Science teacher? I've seen him get a quick look at different girls sometimes.

Aretha – Yeah, he might look sometimes but he's too smart to touch.

Mai – Why do you say that?

Aretha – Well one time he was tutoring students after school and he would sit next to each person and have what he called a five-minute conference. Well, when he sat next to me, I accidentally, on purpose, placed my hand on his knee.

Mai – No way!

Aretha – Yes I did.

Mai – Then what happened?

Aretha – Then I slowly ran my hand up his leg, his thigh, near his crotch.

Mai – Oh no! What happened?

Aretha – Nothing.

Mai – Ah, come on. You always wearing those low-cut blouses with your bits halfway falling out. You're rubbing his leg. You can't tell me that nothing happened.

Aretha – Well I didn't feel a thing but his mushy leg. I mean he must not have any muscles and absolutely nothing was hard. I was bored and thought about moving my hand to his other leg. He then must have had a premonition because he slowly moved his leg, I think he crossed the left leg over to the right one, and shifted the textbook so that it pushed my hand away and then he said "I want you to focus on getting at least an A or B in this class. Just like I said the first day of school, everybody should get an A or B." He then said, "I'm an old man. I've been around a long time. I can help you if you want but you have to do the right thing just as I must always do the right things". And then, I swear, he looked me dead in the eye, and I mean he looked at me like nobody else has ever looked at me.

Mai – How so?

Aretha – Well, [*pause*] it's like he looked deep into my eyes. It's like he touched my inner being and I don't even know anything about these kinds of feelings. Well, he looked at me, and his eyes kind of twinkled.

Mai – Get outta here. What are you saying?

Aretha – I'm explaining it the best way I can. His eyes twinkled, I don't know, like Santa Claus.

Mai – What?

Aretha – Yeah. It was like some type of nonverbal communication. It was like he was saying "Thanks for the compliment but I am too old. Now let's just focus on learning".

Mai – Are you psychic now?

Aretha – I don't know. All I know is that I could read his mind at that point in time and I felt my inner self for the first time.

Mai – Did you ever go in for round two?

Aretha – No way! I got the message. People think that teachers mess around with the students. I think they call them prey or predators, but in reality, I bet that it is less than 1% of teachers who do it with kids. I mean, it's too dangerous. They could go to jail and lose their jobs.

Mai – Or get STDs.

Aretha – Yep, that's a sentence worse than jail if it's incurable.

BOY FROM THE MOON

[Act III: Scene 1. Rachel and Tina are having a conversation in the hallway of the high school when Antonio interrupts.]

Antonio – Science location where?

Tina – Now Tony, you know where it is. Science is in the same room today as yesterday.

Antonio – Follow you me. OK. Don't get lost me. OK.

Tina – Sure. Sure. But Tony, *[pause]* just follow us like a good lap dog.

Tony – OK.

[Antonio walks behind Tina and Rachel as they proceed to the Science lab.]

Rachel – You understand him? Is he some kind of nut or retard?

Tina – Naw... see Tony realizes that he can't hang out with the jocks *or* the nerds. I mean look at him. He's not a hunk, so football is out. He's too short for basketball. He's too skinny for wrestling. He can't swim, dance, play baseball, volleyball, or a musical instrument. He's not smart enough to be with the super nerds with all their 'AP' classes. So moon boy decided to be unique and memorable. He has created his own persona. He created his own language with its own syntax in order to be outstanding. You see, he sorely needs to be noticed.

Rachel – That's just about everybody in high school. Some kids dye their hair purple and orange to get attention. So he created his own type of language?

Tina – Well, just listen. Analyze his sentence structure and choice of words. Instead of pronouncing "th" like the rest of us, he uses the letter "d". So when he says "dem, dat, and doz" ….

Rachel – Yeah, I get it. That represents them, that, and those. I've even heard famous people say stuff like "Da Bulls" and "Da Bears" when referring to the sports teams in Chicago.

Tina – Right. So Tony is not all that unique, but he's cute. And when he says a word that begins with a "w" he supplants it with a "v". Therefore "was" equals "vas," witch becomes "vitch," worried transforms into "vorried," and so forth and so on.

Rachel – Wow. You should study languages. I mean the UN, the United Nations, could use a Multilanguage linguistic translator. If you figured this out on your own, just for fun, just think what you could accomplish with formal training. You could probably learn French, Spanish, Italian, and Portuguese easily because they all have common roots. I think it's called Latin etymology. And then you could probably study Japanese, Chinese, and Korean simultaneously because I'm sure they all have similarities.

Tina – Well thanks a lot for volunteering me for all this extra credit. I' m taking Latin this semester and I noticed that they usually have the main verb at the end of the sentence.

Rachel – Then that must be where moon boy got the idea. He's probably taking Latin, you know, at a different time than you.

Tina – Yeah, you're right. I have it 2nd period, so he must have it later and came up with this creative language idea. I like the way he never curses. He changes a letter or two, but you still get the drift.

Rachel – Yeah, I remember when someone stepped on his foot, and he shouted, "Vitch!"

Tina – Yep, and the teacher couldn't suspend him for cursing, but everybody knew what he meant.

Rachel – Yeah, and if we just start focusing on life, there are no limits to our potential. With your knack for languages, you could have an important job with the FBI, CIA, or just a mega-business entity. You could be making half a mil a year with your skills.

Tina – I don't possess those skills now. We're still in dreamland. In reality we are still in high school.

Rachel – Yeah, I know, but you have to dream, plan, inspire yourself and focus on the unlimited possibilities. You can be what you want to be if you work hard and prepare yourself. This is America. All things are possible. Remember in Lit class we had to pick an author who inspired others. The teacher gave us a list of famous motivators. I picked Horatio Alger and you picked Norman Vincent Peale. These people wrote books that inspired others to be millionaires and billionaires.

Tina – Yep, you're right. It's amazing how you can relate to that school stuff and make it seem so simple and real. It's like you make old history come alive.

Rachel – Well I can't take all the credit. My 7th Grade Social Science teacher, Mr. Zid, was a real weirdo. He would come into class differently each day.

Tina – How so?

Rachel – When he introduced people from history like Paul Revere, Benedict Arnold, or John Brown, he gave such vivid interesting examples. I mean before we studied the Revolutionary War, he read to us a poem entitled "Paul Revere's Ride", I think it was by Henry Wadsworth Longfellow, but I'm not sure. I do remember he had corny jokes like "You must be a poet 'cause your feet show. Look at them; they're long fellows". That's how I remember stuff, because he was so goofy. I mean he was a smart teacher, but kind of weird. After he read us the poem about Paul Revere, he then went back and explained every line. He would ask us a question about each line – a phrase, a word, or an historical allusion. He would give us about 2 seconds to answer. If no one could answer the question, he would then answer his own question and move on to the next line. We were supposed to take notes because what he was telling us would be on an upcoming test. Nobody could keep up with him. I remember one parent came to school to bitch and moan about his teaching style. They went to the principal and said that he treated us 7th graders like we were high school seniors. He didn't budge. He didn't care if parents complained and whined to the administrators. In fact, he told my mom right in front of me that students today weren't challenged enough and they had it too easy.

Tina – I see why you call him weird. Sounds like you had a good time.

Rachel – We had a great time! Like when he reviewed Paul Revere's ride, the poem, Mr. Zid dressed up in this old-fashioned outfit. The big hat, funny looking trousers, shirt that looked like a lady's blouse with ruffles … the whole get-up.

Tina – Unreal.

Rachel – He captivated our attention. He entertained and challenged us.

Tina – Cool.

Rachel – Yeah, Mr. Zid said we have so many discipline problems because kids have it too easy. We have too much idle time. He told my mom that the kids in his classroom always sit in groups of five at tables. Therefore one student could take notes about the first line of the poem, the next student could take notes from the second line, and so on. Later, after class, they could pool their resources and notes and consolidate all of the facts. He said kids need to work together to solve problems. He called it collaboration. And the best part was when he explained the entire poem about Paul Revere, but he talked so fast that only a few kids could keep up with him

Tina – Yeah, probably those apple polishers who got straight A's. But wow, you had a great teacher in 7th grade. He sounds so inspirational.

Rachel – Yep, he was, but guess what, he was later fired.

Tina – Get outta town. Why would they fire somebody like that? He sounded so good.

Rachel – Well there were a lot of reasons. First, I heard that other teachers were jealous of him because he showed them up. We would be laughing and learning at the same time. I heard he had a personality conflict with the assistant principal.

Tina – Oh yeah. I have seen some principals and assistant principals that are real witches.

Rachel – I remember one day we were in class on the third floor. We were bustin' out laughing. Mr. Zid was laughing so hard he was crying. Well, the door opened and the assistant principal called him over, wondering what the heck was going on. You should have seen him. You know how someone looks when a vicious dog is about to attack them. Think about a Rottweiler or a pit bull. Well Mr. Zid looked at her and calmly said that we were just relating to the Prohibition Era in the 20s and making connections to the marijuana debate today, you know, should weed be made legal. Well Mrs. AP (the assistant principal) was pissed. I mean we could sense and feel how relaxed and confident he was. He made no excuses or apologies. It was like he was in an attack-mode but didn't attack. He said quite calmly what we were doing. Well then, Mrs. AP, said that the class needs to discuss and debate issues in a quieter manner so as not to disturb the other rooms.

Tina – Yeah, the other boring, deadpan rooms.

Rachel – Wow! That deadpan image hit the spot. That gives me the image of a patient in the hospital with a funky bedpan that needs to be cleaned out.

Rachel – Gross and thanks, but getting back to the situation, not only did he have these conflicts with the principal and assistant principal regarding his teaching methods, but I heard that he didn't get fired, he just up and quit. Someone said he didn't feel like teaching anymore and was planning to retire and write a book.

Tina – Now where did you get this juicy gossip? Are you making this all up?

Rachel – No. He would to talk to everyone. I mean he would laugh and joke with the security guards, the lunchroom ladies, the janitors or custodians, the teachers, parents, and the kids.

He wasn't stuffy like some teachers, trying to keep a mean face all year long.

Tina – Yeah, like Mrs. Pritchard who looks like she had prunes and nails for breakfast every day. They say the only day she cracks a smile is on the last day of school in June.

Rachel – That's so true. But Mr. Zid wasn't like that. Like I said he would laugh and joke with everybody, every day.

Tina – Well maybe he did quit. I heard that people who write books can make a lot of money, especially if it becomes a movie.

Rachel – Right. Look at those Harry Potter books. Mr. Zid told us that the lady who wrote them, Ms. Rowling, I think that's her name, well anyway she used to be on welfare and one day she decided to write a book called Harry Potter and the rest is history. One Harry Potter book after another and then one movie after another.

Tina – Yeah, sometimes I hate those types of books. I mean sometimes it's nice but sometimes it's boring and predictable. It's like some of those dumb action movies. You know the hero is going to win or overcome all obstacles, so what's the point?

Rachel – The point is making money, having fun, keeping your audience entertained and filled with suspense.

Tina – So the lady who created Harry Potter is rich? She made a lot of money?

Rachel – Yeah. Mr. Zid said she was filthy rich. A billionaire. The only woman in England richer than she is the Queen of England.

Tina – My goodness! No wonder Mr. Zid quit teaching. He had dreams of being rich.

Rachel – Well, maybe yes and maybe no. There were all sorts of rumors on why he left. Oh yeah, I also heard he got fired because he wasn't certified and needed a couple of classes for some kind of endorsement.

Tina – Oh, now, come on. This is beginning to sound like some kind of Sherlock Holmes or Hardy Boys mystery. I need to put on my sleuth-suit and work on this case. Missing a couple of classes? That sounds totally ludicrous. Why would they fire somebody who was a great teacher, somebody who related boring history lessons and made them come to life? I mean, why fire somebody who is not *trying* to do his job but was really doing an outstanding job just because he was short two or three education classes.

Rachel – Hey, I don't know. They say the public school system is messed up. My mom told me that it was worse when she was in school.

Tina – How could it have been worse? It sounds like numbskulls are running it.

Rachel – Well she said it was like the Keystone Cops when she was young. They had one program for learning, then two years later another program came out, and then two years later another program was started. And then two years later, guess what?

Tina – Another new program?

Rachel – Worse. They went back to the first program. Around and around in circles. Like a Merry-Go-Round.

Tina – The more things change, the more things stay the same.

Rachel – My mom said that one day somebody challenged all these new reforms and said that we need to get back to the basics because kids can't read, write, or do basic math equations.

Tina – Who were the Keystone Cops?

Rachel – My mom would rent these ancient movies from the library, she called them the classics. All of the movies were in black and white and some of them didn't have sound. Well, these policemen would run around in circles instead of directly chasing down criminals. They would bump into each other, hit each other, poke fingers and blame one another.

Tina – How could you look at a movie with no sound? You won't know what's going on.

Rachel – Yeah, well these movies were created at the beginning of the movie industry. Nobody invented sound yet. When somebody did create it, they called them "talkies". So before the "talkies" they had soundless movies with words at the bottom of the screen.

Tina – Oh like the subtitles in a foreign film.

Rachel – Yep, only every movie in America back in the 1920s had subtitles. Nobody talked. I think the movie theater was called a *Nickelodeon* because it only cost a nickel to see the movie.

Tina – Heck, that about all it was worth.

Rachel – Oh, keep in mind the cost of living and the rate of inflation. I mean, a nickel back then was probably like going to the show today and spending $5.

Tina – What?

Rachel – Yeah, a penny could get you a cup of coffee or a big candy bar. But getting back to my point about the Keystone Cops

Tina – Oh yeah, I see your mom's point. The teachers were running around in circles, creating all these new programs, and the kids weren't learning.

Rachel – Right. And then someone said these kids need to go back to the basics, which is learning to master Reading, Writing, and Arithmetic, which was nicknamed years ago as the 3 R's

Tina – I'm lost again. Why the 3 R's?

Rachel – Well it seems corny, maybe Mr. Zid was around back then, but it represented Readin', 'Ritin, and 'Rithmetic.

Tina – OMG! That is super corny.

Rachel – Yeah, but that's why now we have so many standardized tests to move up to the next grade and to graduate. We have all those darn special tests for Reading. We have a Writing Mastery Test where you have to write as essay that fills up four pages with thoughts about a dumb passage. And we have those stupid Basic Skills Math Tests that nobody seems to master.

Tina – Don't remind me. All those important tests stress kids out.

Rachel – I know.

Tina – I know of some kids who are real smart and they just freeze up and fail the major tests, but they get all As and B's throughout the school year. One teacher called it some kind of anxiety reaction.

Rachel – What's that?

Tina – I'm not positive but it's like you freeze up, like stage-fright. Let's say you rehearse for a school play. You know your lines. You've practiced every day. But the day of the actual performance, when the curtain goes up, the lights come on, the music plays, and you are on center stage with hundreds or maybe thousands of people staring at you, like they can see the bottom of your tonsils, you totally freeze up, forget or miss your lines, and feel like a jackass.

Rachel – Yeah, I feel you. I heard some school districts are abolishing the stressful standardized tests because of the pain it causes, sometimes irreversible behavioral and emotional pain. Sometimes they abolish the tests because teachers and principals cheat.

Tina – Yeah I've heard of coaches, teachers, principals cheat to get certain kids through; like I remember Melvin in eighth grade. He was so dumb, but they passed him on.

Rachel – I remember him too. He was always in a fight; I think he did drugs, always acting silly in class.

Tina – Yep. I'm sure somebody cheated to get him through. And sometimes the kids themselves cheat. They pass notes and answers to their friends, send text messages, and I've even seen them do sign language in class that they learned in the hearing impaired class and the teacher had no clue as to what was going on.

Rachel – Yeah, and some teachers let the kids cheat and just pretend not to see. See the teachers' jobs are also at stake. If too many kids fail, the teacher might lose her job.

Tina – So true. I remember my eighth grade Science teacher failed half of the class. I felt that she should have been fired. I mean obviously she couldn't teach and relate to young people.

Rachel – Ditto. That's why I couldn't figure out why Mr. Zid got fired or laid off. The kids who failed his class, and it was not many, caused their own failure. Take Ronald. He didn't do any work from September till June. Carl was sleep or sleepy every day. Judith daydreamed about her boyfriends all day.

Tina – Yeah and Marsha was high from the night before.

Rachel – And Yolanda must have stood in the food line in heaven when brains were being passed out.

(*Both girls laughing hysterically*)

Tina – I heard she went back for seconds and thirds. (*Both girls laughing*)

Rachel – Yeah, she is so dumb that she can't even cook. I mean, not even microwave.

Tina – What? As big as she is?

Rachel – Yeah, I'm serious. I went to her house a couple of times and she never mentioned cooking, only going to some fast food places. So one day I asked her. I wasn't trying to be sarcastic, but I said in a nice way, "Girl you are so healthy looking - 'cause you know that is the politically correct phrase now, healthy or full-figured. So I say to her, "You are so healthy-looking, yet you are always eating some fast food. Don't you ever cook?"

Tina – What did she say to that?

Rachel – Well she looked perplexed and embarrassed, so I added "You know cooking is an art form, it's even fun experimenting with new ideas. I thought you would love to try new recipes. Then she broke down and cried. She said "It's too difficult. It's too hard. You have to read. You have to be able to read. You have to measure stuff like in Math class. You have to remember stuff, and tell time, and subtract." *[pause]* Then she burst into a type of moan and tears were streaming down her face like Niagara Falls. I felt so bad. I knew she was so slow but this was a revelation.

Tina – Aw, man, now I'm sorry I mentioned Yolanda. I knew she was dumb but I never thought anybody could be that dumb.

Rachel – Well let's be fair. Maybe we shouldn't call her dumb.

Tina – Oh here you go with that politically correct crap.

Rachel – No, this is not crap. Yolanda is not necessarily dumb, perhaps unknowledgeable, or underexposed in some areas

Tina – Unknowledgeable in many areas and overexposed in regards to body fat.

Rachel – Well so are you. I mean ignorant of things. So am I. Everybody knows some things and everybody, and I mean everybody in the whole wide world can learn and take lessons.

Tina – Take lessons on what?

Rachel – Take lessons on anything. Like I said earlier you should take foreign language lessons cause you a have a knack for it. Everybody can learn something. Even the President of the United States isn't a know-it-all.

Tina – Ok. I'll humble myself. Please accept my apology.

Rachel – There is no need to apologize. Let's just not be too critical and judgmental of others. People need to focus on their own problems and their own shortcomings and not spend time, no, perhaps, I should say spend *no time* thinking about the faults of others. Take a good look in the mirror first. Meditate on that.

Tina – I get it. Check yourself out first. Criticize no one but you. Remember that song by Michael Jackson. Take a look in the mirror or the man in the mirror.

Rachel – I think they call it introspection.

Tina – Wow! You're deep.

Rachel – Profound!

[Both girls laugh and proceed down the hallway to class.]

PowerPoint Disaster

[Act III: Scene 2. Carlos and Berra are at their lockers in the hallway. Berra, nicknamed Bear, a big guy that looks like a football linebacker, is visibly upset.]

Berra – I'm going to bust that hoe Jasmine in the mouth, Joe.

Carlos – Slow your roll, G. What happened?

Bear – Man, I spent an hour working on my power point presentation for Mrs. Powers. I had that stuff down pat. I had info embedded in every picture. Man, the slides were raw.

Carl – So, what about Jasmine?

Bear – Man that ho turned off the computer. You see. I saved my stuff on the computer and then went to my French class. I returned to the computer lab on lunch to finish my project. Jazzy was on my computer so I asked her to get off.

Carl – So she didn't feel that she should get up. Is that it? Were there other computers available? I mean, it wasn't really your computer; it was the school's property.

Bear – Okay, so it wasn't my personal computer, but my stuff was on there. There was only one available computer and it was only two workstations away from her.

Carl – So why didn't she get up?

Bear – She was doing some stupid stuff with those Barbie dresses. You know, they change the dresses. Man, I asked her politely to get up.

Carl – So she wouldn't give it up.

Bear – Yeah, she kept saying "Just a minute, just another minute." And when that minute was up, she would say "Just another minute."

Carl – Yeah, that's aggravating, but she was on the computer first. It was her class because you said that you were on lunch.

Bear – But my stuff was on the computer! I'm doing work for a Social Science project. She was just playing around.

Carl – Why didn't you save it on a flash drive?

Bear – I didn't have one.

Carl – Why didn't you ask someone and borrow theirs?

Bear – Man, people around here are *so* selfish. They don't want to loan you anything. In fact, they're happy to see you up a creek with no paddle.

Carl – That's whack, but I guess so true.

Bear – Yeah, so this Jazzy was aggravating me on purpose. So after I asked her repeatedly and nicely, she finally said "OK" and got up.

Carl – So why are you so pissed?

Bear – Because that ho turned off the computer when she got off. All she had to do was close out the program, but this witch shuts off the computer and all the previously saved materials were lost.

Carl – Couldn't you have opened up the C drive or something and retrieved the information?

Bear – I tried that and everything was lost. I checked the computer drive, the control panel, everything.

Carl – Was Jasmine sorry and apologetic?

Bear – Naw, she was smiling and laughing. She kept saying that I was stupid for not saving it on a flash drive.

Carl – I see, so she was rubbing salt into an open wound.

Bear – Yeah, and loving it!

Carl – Well it can't be all bad. All you have to do is remember what you wrote and put it with the right pictures.

Bear – That's the problem. I don't remember the exact words. I was just writing; the flow took control. I was summarizing info from various sources about the Nazis. Now I have to go back and research all that stuff again and summarize it again.

Carlos – Well, life is a series of events. A series of mistakes and opportunities. You now have the opportunity to recreate what you wrote, perhaps it will be better. This could have been a blessing in disguise.

Berra – Thanks for nothing! I don't need those kinds of blessings.

Carlos – You never know. Live and learn. Don't get so uptight. You made a mistake. You didn't save your work. Don't be mad at Jazzy for your errors.

Berra – But she was wrong for doing what she did. I'm going to get even with that witch!

Carlos – Man, don't start. Stop tripping. If you do something, then she will retaliate and do something else. Then you will do something else. Then her. Then you again. On and on. A vicious cycle of evil will ensue. Both of you might get suspended. One of you might bring a gun to school to end it. Your life will be wasted, ruined, or be over all because of some little stupid thing. Live and let live.

Berra – I guess you're right, but I'm still pissed.

[The roaring bear's temper has abated. Carlos and Berra now walk calmly toward their class.]

Too Damn Good

[Act IV: Scene 1. The doorbell rings in the home of Arthur's parents. Artie goes to the door and greets Berra. Art sits on the couch while Berra sits on the recliner.]

Berra – I'm going to have to break up with Rachel.

Arthur – Why? You two seem like the perfect couple.

Berra – We are far from perfect. The main problem is that she talks too much.

Art – Man, that's what girls do. All of them talk too much. One of my boys told me that he's breaking up with his girl because she always wants to talk and text on the phone.

Bear – Well Rachel talks too much about me. What we do in private should stay private.

Art – Like the phrase, "What's done in Vegas stays in Vegas?"

Bear – Yeah. I believe that every date we've had, every moment we have been together, has been witnessed by all her girlfriends. It's gotten to the point that when the two of us are together, I can feel the presence of twenty other people in the room. It's like a horror movie.

Art – How so? You might be paranoid or something.

Bear – I can give you concrete examples and then you tell me if I am paranoid. One day I'm at her crib. She doesn't want to go out or look at movies. She says, "Let's play *Scrabble*."

Art – The word game. That sounds boring.

Bear – It can be a lot of fun if you are playing with someone you love or someone who is a lot of fun. I said, "OK, let's play

100

for fun." Then she gets out some rule book and reviews which person goes first, how many letter tiles are distributed, and the consequences for challenging your opponent on word choices.

Art – What is this challenge thing?

Bear – If a player puts down a word and your opponent doesn't believe that it is an acceptable word, the challenger examines a dictionary. If the word is not in the dictionary, you then get an extra turn. But *[pause]* if you challenge your opponent and the word is real and in the dictionary, they, your opponent, get the points and an extra turn because you just lost a turn. They could then end up with more points and win.

Art – I don't understand the purpose of points. You said that you wanted to play for fun.

Bear – You're right. I just wanted to have some fun with my girl, but like I said, she got out this rule book and she wanted to keep score. Sometimes if you land on a double word points square or a triple letter points, you can rack up a lot of points and win the game. So we played for a while and she puts down these crazy words that I never heard about.

Art – Well all she has to do is put the word in a logical sentence. That should give you a clue to its authenticity.

Bear – Normally I would say that you are right. That sounds logical. But she can't put the word in a sentence or provide a definition. For example, she puts the word "Qat" down. Now the letter "Q" is on a triple point square so I challenge her word choice. She just laughs and says she can't either put the word in a sentence or provide a definition. Then she asks me do I challenge her. I reply, "Hell yeah, you're just making up words."

So she then gets a Scrabble dictionary of acceptable words and it was unbelievable.

Art – Qat is a word?

Bear – Yes. It was acceptable. It was not an abbreviation. I think it is an evergreen shrub that is normally spelled "Kat" but alternate spellings are acceptable. Now I look stupid because she starts this insidious, demonic laugh and chants, "You lose your turn, you lose your turn." She then draws new tiles and makes another ridiculous word. I think it was "fag."

Art – Now I know that "fag" is not acceptable. It is an abbreviation for faggot. Abbreviations aren't acceptable in Scrabble. It is also a derogatory slang term for a homosexual male.

Bear – I'm with you 100%. So I challenge her and the Scrabble dictionary said that it was acceptable.

Art – No way!

Bear – I'm not shushing you. I think that fag means to be weary from labor or work. She then draws more new tiles and makes still another ridiculous word. Now by this time I am too scared to challenge her again because she is armed with this Scrabble dictionary and I don't want to lose another turn. As the game progressed, I did challenge her about four more times, and each and every time she was backed up by the dictionary.

Art – She sounds like a pool shark hustling a novice. I see that she may be an obsessive compulsive player who takes the game too seriously, but how does this relate to her talking too much.

Bear – OK. Here's the thing. While we are playing, I think it was our third game, her girlfriend Alice calls. Alice has a lot of men problems so they talk all the time. Alice must have talked for less than a minute when Rachel tells her, in a loud and excited voice, "I'm sorry about your situation girl but I'm having so much fun kicking Bear's butt at Scrabble." She then goes on to say, "I thought that he was *so* smart, being on the B Honor Roll every year at school, planning to go away to college and be a lawyer, but I just whipped him at Scrabble three times in a row and I'm kicking his ass right now."

Art – Man, that's cold-hearted. She busted you out in front of her homey.

Bear – Not only is she as cold as dry ice, but what we do together, our intimate moments in each other's embrace, should not be broadcasted to her girlfriends.

Art – She's not only broadcasting your relationship, she's putting you down for her girls. It's like she needs to put you down in order to build herself up. That's sick.

Bear – You see my point. Thank you. A woman should support her man and make him feel good. I didn't care that she won, in fact I was happy to see her so happy. My whole mission in the relationship is to make her happy, especially in the sex arena. It's a reciprocal thing. I make her happy and she in turn makes me happy. But her actions during this game revealed a part of her personality that I never saw before. She was so aggressive and cruel, gloating over her achievements. This is just one example that I know she talks about me too much.

Art – I have heard about women who talk about their man behind their back, but she busted you out right in front of your face.

Bear – She talks about me behind my back too. Her parents know that we are kicking it. Her mom calls me "Son." I have a key to the house. Well, one day, it must have been on a Saturday because Rachel fixed me breakfast. It was so nice – pancakes, eggs, bacon, and fruit cocktail. I gave her a little peck, a brief kiss because her parents were still home. I then told her that I had something to do. I forget now where I was going, but that's not the point. We said our goodbyes and I left the house. As I was driving down the road, I remembered that I left something on the kitchen table that I needed. I don't remember exactly what it was but it was very important. Maybe it was my scientific calculator. I drive back to the house and enter through the kitchen door. I have my own key so I didn't have to knock or ring the bell. When I entered I could hear Rachel talking about me on the phone to one of her ex-boyfriends.

Art – She's gossiping about you to her ex?

Bear – Yeah, I heard her mention his name in the conversation. I'm not going to say his real name, so I'll just call him Joe. She says, "That's what I like about you Joe, you weren't stuck up and sensitive like Bear is."

Art – She got specific?

Bear – Grossly specific! She goes on and on about my frailties and puffs up Joe's ego. I was so hurt. She then says, "I know that we won't ever get back together but …." That's when she saw me entering the living room. I didn't want to hide in the kitchen any longer. I wanted her to see me listening to her. I asked her, "What's going on?" She then told Joe, "I'll have to call you back because something has come up." She hangs up the phone and justifies her actions.

Art – How could a woman justify demeaning you to her ex-boyfriend?

Bear – She did it. She said that she was just venting. She said that they were just friends now without any sexual encounters. They were *not* friends with benefits. She said that she needed another man's perspective on relationships and that he was a true friend.

Art – But she's talking to him like he is one of her girlfriends. She's probably telling him all of your business. She's even comparing his previous performance to your current actions. I see what you mean. There is no privacy in your relationship. Women say that men hold too much in and that we don't talk enough about what's inside us. But she is the total opposite. She talks too darn much.

Bear – Yeah, and it gets worse.

Art – Oh no! How could it be any worse?

Bear – Sometimes, at school, when I'm walking to my locker, I notice a group of girls looking at me. They don't just look. They giggle and smile. They give me the eye. On one occasion, one girl spread her hands out to signify ten inches and another girl corrected her by spreading her hands out to represent twelve inches. They all then looked at me and laughed.

Art – So you believe they were talking about you?

Bear – I know Rachel tells *everybody* everything. My privates aren't even private. One girl, a reputed gangbanger, came up to me one day and boldly said, "When are we going to hook up?" I said, "Excuse me but I'm dating someone." Now Sarah, I don't think you know her, hangs with the Devil's Hell Raisers. Sarah said, "I know you're dating Rachel. That's cool. I don't want to date you. I just want to kick it once in a while. No commitments. No strings attached. No dating. Just fun once in a while".

Art – That could be dangerous.

Bear – Tell me about it. First, Rachel is going to find out. Then the whole school is going to find out. And the folks are going to hate my guts. You don't mess with one of their witches unless you have been initiated into the club. I don't want that.

Artie – Yeah, and if you don't join, they'll harass you forever. I know of a guy that got on their hit list and he suffered dearly for it. One day he had four flat tires on his car. Another day, about a month later, he had a smashed car window. A month later, after he got his window fixed, he came out of the house and realized that he had two smashed windows. They can be ruthless.

Berra – That's my dilemma. If I mess with Sarah, I'm screwed. If I try to ignore her after that bold proposition, I'm screwed. All of this because Rachel talks too much.

Arthur – And also because you're too damn good.

Not ready to be Tied Down

[The doorbell rings. *Arthur goes to the door and greets Saeykun. Berra says his goodbyes and exits. Arthur and Saeykun then sit on the couch in Arthur's living room sometime in the evening. Arthur is looking at various video games trying to decide upon which one to play first.]*

[Saeykun has a worried look on his face. His brow is so wrinkled that it looks like farmers could plant carrots in the rows.]

Saeykun – Man, my girl is starting to give me the look.

[Arthur, still fumbling with the game choices, doesn't look up, but responds.]

Arthur – What is *the look*?

Sae – That's the look women give you when they want to talk about something that troubles them. It's a look that says, "I have something very important to ask you" or "We need to talk about your problem." It's a look that opens the door to individual exposure. It's when they look into your eyes hoping to get in touch with your soul.

[Art puts the games down. Now his curiosity is whetted. He turns and faces Sae, sits on the edge of the davenport, focusing now all of his attention on Saeykun.]

Artie – Man, I never thought about that before. When dames give me that look, I immediately look the other way.

Sae – You're a smart man. But sometimes you need to find out what's troubling them if you are in a relationship. If you have a good thing going on, you want to keep it going on. You don't want to lose your girl because of selfishness.

Artie – I see your point.

Sae – Well my girl gave me *the look* the other day so I ask, "What's wrong baby?" She then unloads her dream about us getting married.

Art – Dude, you're only seventeen. [*Sae nods his head in agreement.*] Why is she stressing you about marriage?

Sae – Well, we've been dating for two years. I don't see or want to see anyone else. Neither does she. Sex is too dangerous.

You know, all the STDs out there. Life is too short to waste it on killer sex. So we committed ourselves to each other. We made a pledge to be faithful to each other and I trust her with my whole heart. But I have plans. I plan to graduate in three months from high school and go away to college. I'm very good in mathematics and computer science. I plan to be an electrical engineer or a computer analyst.

Art – I see you have plans, but she has plans also. Seventeen is a pretty young age to get married. I can see some benefits; well really, I can see very few benefits of getting married so young. If you love her, it can work out, but your goals of going to college and becoming an engineer could be lost forever.

Sae – I know. She starts quoting statistics about marriage and divorce from the Internet. If 60% of those who marry young get divorced, she looks at the 40% who remained married. She showed me examples of people in their eighties and nineties who got married when they were very young and they are still married today.

Art – Wow, she's smart.

Sae – Yeah, and interesting. One man said that he was married over fifty years because he knew that the woman he married was the one.

Art – How did he know that?

Sae – He said that he prayed and God gave him the answer. He was only eighteen at the time so he had to get his parents' permission to marry.

Art – Yeah, I heard that girls could marry at eighteen but guys are supposed to wait until they're twenty-one.

Sae – Yeah, that's whack! We can join the Army and die in a war but we can't get married. But anyway, he said that he didn't go to church or anything. He just prayed every night and somehow God told him that the girl was the right one.

Art – Well, after fifty years, I guess God was right.

Sae – But he wasn't the only one or the only couple. Another man said that he had been married for more than seventy years. He didn't mention God. He just said that he felt that his wife was the right choice many years later.

Art – I see. Your girl is presenting you with facts, real life experiences, and real examples.

Sae – That's why I love her. She's smart, witty, funny, and logical. Think about it, most people would focus on the 60% rate of divorces, but she looks at the 40% who remained married. It's like that phrase, "Is the glass half full or half empty?"

Art – Yeah, she sees the glass as half full. She's an optimist.

Sae – Exactly. But I'm in a dilemma. I don't want to break up with her, but I'm not ready for marriage. When women give up that look, it's do or die. It's like they lead you into a corner, you feel like a rat in a trap or a maze, and there is no way out. I think that's what they call a Catch-22 situation. Heads you lose and tails you lose. If I marry her, I lose out on my dreams and goals. If I go away to college, then I lose her.

Art – You said earlier that she was smart and logical. Are these the manipulations of a smart, logical girl?

Sae – Maybe. Art, women are smarter than men. I think they are inherently smarter. She is aware of my plans. She plans to include herself in my life. Maybe she's afraid that when I go away to college I will meet someone new. She wants to dig her talons into me like an eagle does her prey. Women – you can't live with them and you can't live without them.

Art – I thought *you* were smart and logical. Your emotions are now making illogical statements. You said men can't live with women or without them. That's illogical and a bunch of horse manure. That's what men do in life – they either live alone without women or they live with them and deal with the consequences. You also said that women are inherently smarter than men. That's another heap of crock. They are no smarter or dumber than we are. Each woman must stand on her own merits. You can't generalize about women. Some women are smart and some are dumb, just as some men are smart and others are dumb. You also said that you will lose out on your dreams of going to college and be an engineer if you marry early. Hogwash! A lot of people get married, have children, and go to college. That's why they have night school. They have classes solely on the Internet so you don't ever go to class, just work on your leisure time. I know of one college that advertises that one can take one class at a time, like one per semester, so you don't get stressed out and feel pressured. You sound like you're getting stressed because you don't have all the facts. Investigate. Check out your options! Don't let your emotions cloud your judgments.

Sae – Man, that's why you are my best friend, you keep it real. I think if a guy has one best friend, then he is blessed. If he has more than one, he is doubly blessed.

Art – I guess that's why when men get married they always have a best man at their side.

[Art smiles and even gloats over his sage advice.]

So are you going to tell her it's over because you must pursue your dreams?

Saeykun – I have to meditate on that first. I could include her in my goals; they would just be a little diverted.

Arthur – You don't have to make rash decisions. That's a good quality.

Saeykun – I'm going to marinate your wise advice and then let it simmer. I do really love Paddy, but I love my career goals too. I want to make the right decision.

Arthur – Think twice and saw once.

Saeykun – I get it. I remember Mr. J told us that in woodshop class.

[Saeykun grabs his jacket and plans to leave. The doorbell rings.]

Arthur – You leaving? Let me get the door.

Saeykun – Yeah, I have to go.

[Carlos and Richard are at the door and the fellows greet each other.]

Arthur – Take care Sae.

Carlos – Hi and bye Sae.

Richard – What's up Sae?

Saeykun – Take care fellows.

Heartbreaker

[Carlos and Richard enter the home of Arthur's parents. Richard sits on the couch while Carlos is standing, rapping, and bouncing to an inaudible beat. Arthur puts on headphones and listens to music.]

Carlos –   Man, I don't talk smack
I slam them down like dominoes
After they lay on their backs
I say "Adiós y Va manos"
Slam, bam, thank you ma'am
You may weep, but I gots to creep.

Richard – Man, what are you spitting? I likes that. That's down! You know Spanish?

Carlos – Oh, you heard me. Naw, I just make stuff up. I was getting my thoughts together. Like Senora Gomez, the Spanish teacher said, just go with the flow. You know, she knows, She was born in "May ee koh". She said don't worry about being wrong. My girl broke up with me so I was getting my head together.

Richie – I thought that *you* were the player. Why did you let a girl break up with you? You *then* look like a chump. You're supposed to kick *her* to the curb and make her beg. I love it when girls beg to have me take them back. Then when I do, I just treat them like dirt 'cause they're used merchandise, used goods, ready for the resale shop.

Carl – Naw, you got it ass-backward. You let the girl break up with you. You don't run after her like a whipped puppy dog. If you break up with her, then her feelings get hurt, she seeks revenge, and your life can be a living hell.

Richie – Oh yeah, I remember Mrs. Franklin saying something in English Lit about Shakespeare. Boy, could she relate that boring stuff to us and make it so down. She said Shakes said something about there is no evil like that of a woman scorned. I thing he said "Hell hath no fury like a woman scorned."

Carl – Wow, I didn't know that you paid attention to school. I thought you were always busy texting the shorties.

Rich – I do a lot of that too. But I can do more than one thing at a time. My mom calls it multi-tasking.

Carl – I'm glad that little witch hit the road. My gramps used to sing a song, "Hit the road, Jack, and don't you come back no more, no more, Hit the road Jack, and don't you come back no more."

Rich – You're glad she left? I thought you told me before that she was the best.

Carl – She was the best. But she was also the best liar. She was the best bull-crapper. She was the best pain in the butt.

Rich – Wow, the truth comes out. I thought you really loved her.

Carl- I did love her. I still love her. But you can love someone and still hate the things that they do. Her main problem is that she loved herself too much. Man, she was full of herself.

Rich – She's like Narcissus?

Carl – Who the heck is Narcissus?

Rich – He was some ancient Greek guy who loved himself so much and kept admiring his own beauty in the mirrored reflection in a lake, that a Greek goddess changed him into a flower, the narcissus that showers its love on no one but itself.

So Narcissus or a narcissistic person is one who loves himself or herself, always looking in the mirror, ignoring others.

Carl – Where do you get this stuff from?

Rich – Well, if you would pay attention in school, you could see how interesting education is. I told you that I'm awake in Ms. Franklin's class. This is where we get the word "narcissism."

Carl – Well Aretha was so full of herself that I don't think she is capable of loving another human being. In fact, she doesn't even like dogs or cats. She doesn't have time in her busy schedule to care for another living creature.

Rich – Man, that's cold. So she doesn't have a dog, cat, parakeet, or even fish.

Carl- Nothing, nada, nil, zilch. She doesn't want to care for a pet. I'm telling you she is full of herself.

Rich – From my experience, you can study any subject. It's just like school. If you want an A, you have to find out what the teacher expects, get examples of excellent work so you can emulate it, and be creative in your presentations. You need to study Aretha's moods and personality. Analyze what makes her happy, find out what pleases her, and she will love you in return.

Carl- That sounds so simple. I did study her. That's why I know she's incapable of love. All she loves are material possessions. She has to have the latest jeans, the most expensive perfumes and coach bags, the finest cars. Her daddy bought her a brand new Mercedes. Now we know a lot a kids have Mercedes, BMWs, and other fine rides at our school. We aren't a ghetto school. But most kids' rides aren't brand new. There is nothing wrong with a used luxury car, or should I say one that was previously driven. Luxury is luxury. It doesn't matter if the vehicle is three or four years old. But Aretha has to have the newest and the best of everything. Her daddy spoils her rotten.

Rich – I see your point. It would be hard to keep up with that.

Carl- She wants to eat out at fancy restaurants not just because they have good food, it must also have what she calls 'ambiance'. If I bought her something, she would thank me, wear it one time, and then stick it in her closet or drawer where it would be lost forever.

Rich – Ok, it sounds like you did all you could to provide things for her. What about sexually?

Carl – Man, I'm the heartbreaker. I'm like Iceberg Slim – cold as ice. I can make them feel so good that they crave and beg for more.

Rich – Well, you tried to provide for her and you fulfilled her sexually. So what was missing in her life? Why didn't she love you? Are you saying she will only love material things and not real people?

Carl – I think she never learned how to love as a young child. Boys traditionally love their mothers and little girls love their daddies. I think that she was never a real "Daddy's girl" in the true sense of love. He may work hard and shower her with gifts. He reminds me of the traveling salesman. After working hard on long business trips, he would come home and give his daughter presents. These presents are a substitute for a real, meaningful, loving relationship. That's why she loves material items. You see, her dad probably never spent quality time with her; a time where true love could blossom.

Rich – That's deep. Where do you get this stuff from? These ideas about love and relationships?

Carl – I check out those talk shows on TV. I'm not a TV junkie or guru, but I do flip the stations and tune in when they have interesting topics.

Rich – Yeah, you can learn a lot from TV, but I can just tune in to you when I have concerns. In fact, why don't I just challenge you to one of those games before your mom comes in from work?

[Richard looks over Arthur's collection.]

Carlos – Cool. I'm down. I've got all day. I'm a free man. No ties.

Richard – Well perhaps I should start charging you for professional consultations.

Carlos – Just put it on my tab.

FIRE MR. X

[Carlos and Richard are still in Arthur's home. Richard now places headphones on his ears.]

Arthur – They ought to get rid of Mr. Xavier. He can't teach at all. He couldn't teach a trained seal tricks.

Carlos – You're right! He doesn't explain things right. He should stop, give examples, get input from the students, give practice exercises, and then review. All he does is talk on and on and nobody pays attention to him.

Arthur – Yep, and in my class, kids listen to music on I-pods, text each other on their phones, curse each other out, throw paper balls, hug and kiss in the classroom, and do basically whatever they feel like doing when this "so-called" teacher is explaining something.

Carlos – Same thing in my class. Mr. X gets *so* mad. He tells one person who is acting up to go outside the classroom for a timeout.

Artie – Yeah, that is so childish. I mean that is really elementary.

Carl – Right! They did that crap to us in the third and fourth grade, but when we went to middle school, that strategy didn't work and the teachers had to come up with something different.

Artie – Exactly! That's the problem with Mr. X. He's trying to con us with some childish punishment. Standing outside the room and hanging out in the hallways with the security guards is cool; it's not real punishment.

Carl – Yep. One time I was in the hall so long that the security guard offered me chocolate chip cookies and another time I had a taffy apple.

Artie – No way! You had a nice break.

Carl – It was sweet! After I ate, my mouth was dry, so I asked the guard for a soda. He didn't have any so I had to drink some water.

Artie – What happened next?

Carl – Nothing really. Security just told me to sit in a chair and be quiet. I started talking about the basketball game last night. We got to talking about the game, then about another game, and then we talked about which team would make it to the playoffs.

Artie – So you had a party in the hall.

Carl – Not quite a party, but I did have a nice respite or break away from that goofy Mr. X.

Artie – Yeah. He doesn't know how to relate to teenagers. We are too old for a timeout. We are juniors in high school. He needs to go back to school himself and learn some new strategies on how to deal with young people.

Carl – No. He needs to get fired. Look at our other teachers. Mr. Thompson is so cool and makes everything interesting.

Artie – Yeah, but Mr. X can't emulate Mr. T. He's one in a million.

Carl – I know, but he can still improve a little. Take Mrs. Konig. She's not funny or very exciting, but she is so nice. I mean she's kind like an angel.

Artie – You're right. Everybody either likes her or loves her. She doesn't try to be a comedienne or an entertainer. She just teaches in a simple yet clear manner. She knows how to break things down to your level.

Carl – Yeah, and Mrs. K always apologizes. When something goes wrong or you don't understand something, she will preface her remarks with the words "I'm sorry".

Artie – Yeah, she is one sorry teacher.

Carl – Ha, ha, ha. Yep, but sorry in the right way. I remember when Dashaun walked over to the air conditioner and turned it on. He then closed the window in the classroom and sat down. Mrs. K didn't show any emotions. She simply asked Dashaun to turn the a. c. off because he didn't first get permission. She then told Dashaun that he could turn the air on if he first asked for permission. She kept saying the words "I'm sorry".

Artie – She apologized and *he* was wrong?

Carl – Yeah. It was unreal. She would say stuff like "I'm sorry that you are so warm and everyone else is comfortable. I'm sorry that they have the heat turned up high in this room, but it is November and it is cold outside. I'm sorry that I didn't make the class rules clear to you. I'm sorry that the rules weren't visibly posted in the room as a constant reminder of our correct procedure."

Artie – She said all that? Right there in the classroom? She didn't waste time putting him out in the hall for a timeout or sending him to the Dean. She handled her business and provided an opportunity for other kids to learn proper protocol.

Carl – Man, she said all that and more. She always prefaces her statements with this phrase "I'm sorry". How could you or any student not like a teacher who is so sincerely apologetic. You just feel good being around her.

Artie – So I guess you feel that she is a good teacher like Mr. Thompson?

Carl – She's an excellent teacher! She breaks things down, she never gets mad, she always apologizes to kids, and the best thing is that she makes you feel good about yourself. She never tries to punk you out.

Artie – You're right. I have noticed that when she talks to students, words that repeatedly come out of her mouth are "You're so smart" and "Good for you" and "I knew that you could do it".

Carl – Yep. She is full of praiseworthy comments. It's like she looks for the good in people and ignores the bad.

Arthur – Yep, like the incident with the air conditioner. Most teachers would have been mad, wrote the student up or called home, or done something stupid like curse the kid out. That's why I say they should get rid of Mr. X and fire his stupid butt.

Carlos – Or if they don't fire him, at least give him the opportunity to observe teachers like Mr. T and Mrs. K. If Mr. Xavier saw them in action he might be so embarrassed that might do better or just quit.

Arthur – Yeah, and Mr. Williams and Ms. Freeman ought to quit too. They are always cursing at the kids and trying to embarrass them.

Carlos – I agree, but I also disagree. Mr. Williams only curses in order to relate to the kids. Like when we were watching a documentary about Emmett Till. Mr. Williams said how important the story was to the Civil Rights Movement and he wasn't going to tolerate anybody talking during the movie. He even said, "If your neighbor starts to talk to you or talks on the phone, just turn to them and say "Shut the fluck up 'cause I'm going to ace this next test".

Arthur – I see what you mean. I realize that he didn't really say "fluck" but the other word. He cursed to get his point across.

Carlos – Yeah. He was relating to us. He knows that's how we talk. He's down!

Arthur – I get your point loud and clear.

Carlos – And Ms. Freeman relates to the kids also by cursing and teaching at the same time. Like the time she came into the room and said real loud, "Damn, somebody needs to wash their ass out with soap! When you take a shower, you need to lather up in the crack!"

Arthur – She said all that?

Carlos – All that and more. Man, she is so ignorant, yet so smart. Some kids don't know how to wash up so she doesn't waste time trying to figure out who or why. She doesn't try to be subtle or discreet. She's low-life but right.

Arthur – I'm now beginning to reconsider my opinion. Maybe these teachers shouldn't quit or be fired. Maybe they need counseling or training. They need to observe and learn from each other. Maybe do skits in those teacher workshops.

Carlos – You're right. If we are always supposed to be learning something new, then so should they.

I'm Ready

[Act V: Scene 1. Padma and Mai Ling are sitting in a fast food restaurant after school.]

Padma – I cornered my boyfriend into a higher level of our relationship.

Mai Ling – You two have had an exclusive relationship for more than a year, right?

Padma – It's been more than two years. We *have* had an exclusive relationship. We have committed ourselves to each other. But Saeykun is graduating in a few months and planning to go away to college. He wants to be an engineer.

Mai Ling – Cool. Like on a train? You might get free tickets.

Paddy – No girl, he doesn't want to be that kind of engineer. Sae wants to be an electrical engineer or a computer engineer.

Mai – That's great. My uncle is an engineer and he makes tons of money. He's been at the gas company for more than twenty-five years and he got my cousin a job there.

Paddy – Is she doing well also?

Mai – Hecky yeah! My aunt said that my cousin, Cindy, made more money her first year as an engineer than she, my aunt, makes after twenty-five years of teaching high school.

Paddy – Get outta here. I never knew they made so much money. I want only the best for Sae but I have to be in his life. Sometimes we women have to serve up an ultimatum. We need to let our men know what's on our minds. We can't just sit back passively and let them make all the decisions. Those days are gone. We're not in the 1800s.

Mai – Oh oh. I feel like a history lesson is coming.

Paddy – No, I'm not going to review the women's' liberation movement; you can do that yourself online. I'm just saying that if we want something, let the man know about it. We need to stop hem-hawing, hoping, and praying. If he tries to skirt an issue, then back him into a corner and force his hand. I think that we women think more intensely than men and we have to let them know what's on our minds.

Mai – So you cornered your boyfriend into what?

Paddy – I told him that I was ready to have his baby. I told him that I preferred to get married, but if that wasn't in his plans, no problem. I still want to have at least one child with him.

Mai – Did he freak out?

Paddy – No, he was cool about it. He even joked about the future child being both smart and handsome.

Mai – Are you giving in to the stereotype that Asian-Americans are naturally smart and East-Indians are born beautiful?

Paddy – I don't like stereotypes any more than you do but Sae was only joking around. I must admit though that he is very smart in math and computers and he happens to be a Korean-American. I, on the other hand, come from a long line of beautiful women.

Mai – So how does he feel about children? Marriage?

Padma – His mind is on school and his future career goals. I want him to finish school. I will support him financially, emotionally, and spiritually. I will not interfere with his ultimate goals; I just want to be an integral part of his life. I feel that if he moves across the country, we may end up talking once a week on the phone. If I call him every day, I will probably get his voicemail. When we talk, he'll talk about how stressed he is, how busy he is, and how much work he's doing. I don't want to hear all that crap over the phone. I want to be in his life while he is changing to make it better. I don't plan to lounge around the house and get fat. I have good job prospects and I might take classes in evening school. But having a child is very important to me at this stage in my life.

Mai – But if he's not ready for marriage, what are your plans? I can't see you on welfare.

Paddy – My plans are to work and continue my education. No one has control over the future. If my job doesn't work out, then I will ask for government assistance. Millions of people do it every day. But if I can continue to work, then so be it. What's most important is having this baby in my life now.

Mai – I understand how you feel but maybe you should talk to someone. Maybe a relative like an aunt or an uncle can give you a different perspective. I'm not saying that you are wrong, but perhaps you should seek counsel before making a decision that could change your life forever.

Paddy – You might be right. I am planning to bring an innocent life into this cruel, cruel world. I believe I am right, but I could benefit from unbiased opinions from others.

Mai Ling – Good. Look before you leap.

Padma – Both my dad and mom would have a fit if they knew what was on my mind. I'm certainly not traditional, but sometimes our generation takes on a new direction.

Mai – Yeah, but having a baby with a man who doesn't want it isn't new. That's ancient history.

Paddy – It would shock my parents.

Mai – Is that what this is all about? Shocking your parents? Moving away from your traditional past. Are you a rebel with a cause?

Padma – Maybe, maybe not.

Hardheaded

[Act V: Scene 2. Robert and Ernesto are sitting in the same restaurant at another booth.]

Robert – I think I'm going to dump Tina.

Ernie – Why? She is so fine. Hey, maybe that's a good idea. Now I can try to hook up with her.

Robert – Man you can have her. She's hardheaded.

Ernie – Do you mean that she doesn't listen to you? She probably has a mind of her own. She's not putty or clay that you can mold or shape to your heart's desire. When you say that she is hard-headed do you mean that she is stubborn and obstinate? The kind of person who keeps on doing the wrong thing over and over and never seems to get the message. I think

Einstein said that craziness is doing the same thing over and over and expecting different results.

Rob – Man you are so swift. People often say things and expect the other person to automatically know and feel their intended meaning. I think you hit it on the head when you made that reference to craziness.

Ernie – Is that reason enough to kick her to the curb? A lot of women are crazy and so are men. There are degrees of craziness. Is she ready to be institutionalized? Or is she just a little off and has idiosyncrasies that you don't like?

Rob – I believe she does things that I don't approve of and when I try to help her, she ignores my best intentions. I try to tell her things to improve her life, to improve our lives together. I want a better relationship. When you are seriously involved with someone, you want only the best for them. But if your mate is close-minded and doesn't open up to new possibilities, the relationship becomes stale and boring and is doomed to failure.

Ernie – You two have been seeing each other about a year, right?

Rob – Right! I try to drop hints that she needs to change her way of living. She has these bad habits. They're not as bad as drugs. It's just that she eats too much and eats the wrong foods. I have suggested that we go for long walks or jog. I like to swim and play tennis. I am open to learn new things like golf or horseback riding. I just want her to be more active. Her only hobby is eating. She is too sedentary.

Ernie – Sedentary? What's that?

Rob – Sedentary relates to people who sit around the house too much. They don't exercise enough. Look at our lives. We sit in school about six hours a day. If we aren't actively using our physical bodies after school, the foods that we eat hang on our bodies and stay with us. We have to burn off excess fats through movement. All I want is for her to be actively engaged in *something*. But her response is, "No go." Whatever I suggest is not interesting enough for her. When I suggest that she should exercise and start eating healthier foods, she responds by the words, "I'll give it some thought." At first, I didn't notice the sarcasm in her voice when she said those words. But then I noticed that every time I mentioned something about an active lifestyle, she replied by saying, "I'll give it some thought." One time she said, "That's a real good idea; I'll have to give it some thought." That's when I realized the sarcastic tone and that I was beating a dead horse.

Ernie – Maybe you are overreacting. We all have our faults. We all have shortcomings. Have you looked into the mirror, not the physical one, but the introspective mirror, and examined your life. Do you *really* listen to others? Are *you* open-minded?

Rob – Everybody needs to improve their situation. Nobody's perfect. I don't think that I'm overreacting. We were in a restaurant one day and she ordered fried chicken, onion rings, and mashed potatoes with gravy. I quietly and politely asked her was she sure that was what she really wanted. I only wanted her to think about her decision, that's all. You know, every action has a reaction. You keep eating fatty foods and guess what, you get fat. Well, after I discreetly asked her to reconsider her food choice, she looked at me like *I* was crazy or had cursed her out. I wasn't trying to embarrass her. I was trying to help her. Why is it when a person tries to help someone, that someone gets an attitude? How we can learn and grow if we are not open to suggestions? And the server didn't make matters any better. He looked at me like I was wrong. I'm trying to help my girl and I'm the bad guy. The bad guy is the one who looks the other way. The real bad guy is the one who keeps his mouth shut when the time for truth is upon us. It's like when someone gets mugged on the street and everybody looks the other way. No one wants to get involved with the police to arrest the culprit for fear of retaliation. When you don't speak up for what is right, you, *too*, are the criminal.

Ernesto – I see your point. People do need to speak up if something is wrong. If I am driving down the road and heading towards a cliff, I would appreciate it if someone shouted and stopped me before I hurl myself five hundred feet downward to my death.

Robert – That's what I did. Or what I tried to do. I warned her about her dietary habits. Then she complains and says that I nag her all the time. I think that there is a big difference between showing compassion and concern for the one you love, and irritating and nagging someone all the time.

Ernesto – I guess people think they know everything when in reality they know very little.

Nag

[Act V: Scene 3. Rachel and Tina are in another booth.]

Rachel – My boyfriend is a nag.

Tina – A nag? I heard of old women being nags, but not that hunk of a boy who looks like he is 35 but is only seventeen.

Rachel – A nag is not the same as a hag. I'm not talking about an old woman who looks like a witch.

Tina – I know. I thought a nag was like some married woman who complains to her husband all the time, trying to make him change his ways or do a whole bunch of tasks or chores around the house.

Rachel – That's exactly what I mean. My boyfriend is a nag. He doesn't support my dreams and goals. All he does he nag me about what *he* wants and how he wants me to change so that he can feel better.

Tina – So he's trying to manipulate you.

Rachel – Yeah, I didn't think of it that way before, but you're right. He must be trying to control me because he doesn't approve of what I do. I have to change to keep him happy. He seems to think that the universe revolves around him. At first I thought he was concerned about me, but as I kept thinking about his proposals, everything bounced back to his ego.

Tina – Everything? Can you give me an example?

Rachel – Girl, I can give you hundreds. OK. Let's see. He nags me about my weight. I know that I'm a little heavy, but I've always been. I am a healthy girl. I was weighing about 10-20 pounds over my desired or ideal size when he met me. Lately, he's been nagging me about losing weight. He says, "Let's go to the health club. I have a membership and you can be my buddy. It's free." Or he'll say, "Let's go jogging or walking Saturday morning" or "Let's play tennis or ride bikes at the zoo on Sunday." You see what I mean. He's like a control-freak. Let's do what he wants to do. By coming up with these exercise activities every single day, this is his subtle way of nagging me about my weight.

Tina – But Rachel, a little exercise won't hurt. Some people exercise and never lose weight. I'm inclined to believe that you are overreacting to his good intentions.

Rachel – Are you taking his side? You're supposed to be *my* friend! He doesn't just casually mention exercise jaunts. If we go to the restaurant, he downright embarrasses me. Let me describe a real scenario to you. We are sitting down at a booth with the menus in our hands. The waiter or waitress comes over to ask what we would like to order. Traditionally, they look at the female customer first. As soon as I open my mouth and say, "I would like the triple cheese hamburger with fries" he blurts out "Are you sure you want that?" Now I am totally hurt. Of course I want it, I ordered it. Here he is trying to restrict my diet and embarrass me in front of a total stranger. In fact, the people nearby heard him and they gave a look of embarrassment. The server looks at me, then at him, and politely says, "I can come back in a few minutes if you need additional time to decide." Well *now* I am totally pissed off! I'm not sure if I want to walk out of the restaurant, curse him out, or reorder the same dish to spite him. I've been eating my way for years. Who does he think he is for trying to change me overnight?

Tina – I see your point and I don't think that I'm siding with him against you, but eating all that meat, cheese, and fried foods isn't all that healthy. You may think it's satisfying because you have been programmed and you are in the habit of eating those types of foods. You remember in our Science class when we did research on food types. What you just mentioned are foods that are major contributors to hypertension, diabetes, and high cholesterol. You've heard of this before. Those foods make your heart work harder, strain your lungs, clog your arteries, and make you feel lethargic and sluggish. I'm not siding with him but I am in agreement with health practitioners who would say that a change is needed.

Rachel – So you're saying he's right and I'm wrong. Some friend you are.

Tina – Girlfriend, true friends try to tell the truth. I am not going to agree with everything you say and do if I sincerely believe you are wrong. If you are headed in the wrong direction, a friend should tell you so. If you are doing drugs or drinking excessively, so that your health, both mental and physical is being compromised, then a true friend would bring it to your attention and try to help you make positive changes for the better. I'm saying he's wrong and you're wrong. He's wrong for fronting you off in public. He should have let you continue with your order, let you enjoy your meal, and maybe the next day, casually mention a healthier food choice. What he did was rude and inconsiderate. I hate it when people try to be polite but deep down they have evil motives. He messed up when he said, in front of strangers, "Are you sure you want that?" That was wrong. Of course you were sure. But you are also wrong by not opening up your mind to new experiences. So you have been accustomed to eating certain foods all your life. Everybody is a victim of habit and their environment. There are people who eat raw fish and love it. People eat pork chitterlings, worms, snakes, deer, chicken, cows, and horses. You can eat what you like and still lose weight if you want to.

Rachel – Girl, you got me. You said people eat cows and horses. I've heard about snakes and worms and that other stuff. How gross!

Tina – You think that's nasty. Well those cheeseburgers that you love so much come from dead cows and maybe horses, sweetie. And lobsters look like they are the remote cousins of cockroaches.

Rachel – Ugh! I think that I should become a vegetarian. Tell me, I'm trying to open my mind to new possibilities and experiences. How can I eat all that I want and still lose weight? You have my curiosity perked.

Tina – OK. This is serious and for real. My uncle is from the old country. He doesn't diet or exercise, yet he is the perfect size and he is sixty years old. His weight is so down he should be a supermodel.

Rachel – What's his secret?

Tina – Basically it's eat all the foods that you like one day and eat certain foods the next.

Rachel – It can't be that simple. You mean, I could eat cheeseburgers, pizza, fries, and down it all with milkshakes and still lose weight? Impossible!

Tina – I thought you just said that you would keep an open mind. You can gorge yourself but you have to follow the regimen every other day. For example, if you eat your favorite foods on Monday, then you have to eat only fruit, vegetables, and whole grain breads on Tuesday. Eat an apple instead of a candy bar. Eat two oranges instead of two slices of pizza. On your healthy day you cannot eat snacks other than the healthy foods mentioned. The only drink that is allowed is water. Ice water or regular tap water is ok. On Wednesday, the next day, you can stuff yourself with steak, cookies, cake, ice cream, and lasagna, anything that you like, but on Thursday you must return to the healthy regimen.

Rachel – You know what? What you said makes sense. It's like you are forcing your stomach and digestive system to relax and change. The fruits and vegetables are high in fiber and would improve elimination. I'm so glad I talked with you. I'm going to try that crazy diet.

Tina – Good. But don't forget to exercise. Glad to be of assistance. That's what friends are for.

MAMA JUANITA

[Act V: Scene 4. Lighting now shifts to Aretha and Mai Ling who are sitting in another booth at the neighborhood fast-food restaurant.]

Aretha – Mother Juanita's funeral is this Friday. Did you know about it?

Mai – I knew it was coming up. She died from lung cancer, right?

Aretha – No. She was battling breast cancer, but it was in remission. One of her sons was on the run. He got into a fight with three boys who wanted to rob him. He shot one of them. The person he shot didn't die but his friends were pissed off. They retaliated. They searched all over town for him but they couldn't locate him. I heard the word on the street was that he fled to Wisconsin. Since the boys couldn't even the score, they killed Mama J.

Mai – Was this one of her real sons or one of the many adoptive ones?

Aretha – He was one of the neighborhood adopted kids. You know she took people in like the old lady down the street who takes in stray cats. They say this old lady has at least fifty cats in the house and about twelve or more that stay outside and hang around for food scraps. Well, Mama J was one of the nicest persons in the whole wide world. She was like that nursery rhyme from kindergarten, you know, the old lady in the shoe who had more children than she knew what to do. I heard that her sons and the boys in the hood got a contract out now for her killers.

Mai – Now that's the wrong response. One wrong doesn't deserve another wrong. People should let the police do their job. The courts should put the killer away for life.

Aretha – In an ideal world that might work, but not in today's real world. Some police are crooked. Even if they catch the guy and try to put him in jail, some slick lawyer might get the killer off on some stupid technicality. And if that doesn't happen, then the judge might just give him five years in jail because the jails are overcrowded. With good behavior, he might get out in less than two years. Your life isn't worth much these days.

Mai – But people shouldn't take the law into their own hands. This isn't the Wild, Wild-West where there were vigilantes.

Aretha – What are vigilantes?

Mai – Vigilantes are ordinary people who don't wait on the police or the legal authorities to do their job. In the Wild West, people often would be the judge and jury. They would hang a horse thief, sometimes on suspicion or supposition.

Aretha – Wow! That seems like overreacting; hanging somebody for just stealing a horse. And what if they were innocent? You can't correct that kind of mistake.

Mai – Well back then your horse was like your car today. Say someone carjacks you while you're driving a *Hummer*. Vigilantes would catch the person and hang them in public today so that other criminals would see the consequences of their actions.

Aretha – That's all well and good, but what if someone were falsely accused. You know, a case of mistaken identity. Especially today, with so many people wearing black hoodies and jeans; it's easy to mistakenly accuse someone.

Mai – You're right. That's why today many people are being released from prisons for being falsely accused and incarcerated for years in prison.

Aretha – I've heard of men getting millions of dollars from the state for being deprived of their citizenship.

Mai – Yeah, there are always cases where the police beat a confession out of someone, only to find out later that someone else raped the girl or murdered the victim.

Aretha – Adults are so stupid. They say that we are full of problems but they are down-right retarded. Confessions should be videotaped. Even those interrogations should be taped. With the technology that we have today, I don't see how and I can't think of any logical reason for the police department to not use camcorders.

Mai – Yeah, grownups are so computer illiterate and electronic imbeciles. A few know the basics, but most don't know how to communicate on Twitter, Facebook, Skype, use e-mail, and video conferencing. Some cities have cameras in police cars like camcorders that record the entire scene when an officer pulls over a motorist. I know technology can be expensive, but when I think of the lives of people, the innocent victims of police brutality, and being falsely accused of a crime and wrongfully incarcerated, it makes me sick.

Aretha – Yeah, and what about the people who went to Death Row, died in the electric chair or gas chamber, when they were, in fact, innocent. DNA testing is a relatively new procedure that has cleared hundreds of innocent victims.

Mai – That's why I said earlier that people shouldn't take the law into their own hands and be vigilantes. It's terribly wrong for whomever to have killed Mama J because they couldn't seek retribution on one of her sons, but it is equally wrong to initialize a contract to eliminate her. Two wrongs don't make a right. What if these well-minded people in a vigilante group find the suspected killer, waste him or her, only to find out years later that they executed the wrong individual.

Aretha – I agree, but it is also frustrating to wait on the police to investigate. They don't always care. Sometimes they only go through the formality of an investigation. There are millions of unsolved murders in America.

Mai – One reason for the large numbers of unsolved murders is the uncooperativeness of the community. People are afraid to speak up. People are afraid to cooperate with the police. They're too scared to trick. Retribution by gangbangers is too risky. Like the phrase, "Snitches end up in ditches".

Aretha – But if people don't cooperate with the authorities and they don't take matters into their own hands, what kind of life are we living. No, we aren't really living – we only exist – waiting to be a victim of some merciless action by a deranged individual or group of individuals. We are like the prey in the wild jungle just waiting to be pounced upon by a stronger predator.

Mai – What if you call the police and the thugs vandalize your car the next day? What if they burglarize your home? How can you live in peace always wondering what might happen next?

It's best to live and let live. Ignore the ignorant people. Go to school, get a good job, and move away from the riffraff.

Aretha – That's a cop-out! Good people have to reclaim their neighborhoods. Revolutionary changes begin with one person. A lot of people spoke out against the injustices of racial segregation before Rosa Parks and Dr. Martin Luther King, Jr. There were boycotts in the South before those two made national headlines, but it was the actions of those two people who made history and civil disobedience famous.

Mai – And Dr. King was one person who risked his life to make inequities an international concern.

Aretha – Yep, and Dr. King got his inspiration from people like Mahatma Gandhi and A. Philip Randolph.

Mai – Who were they?

Aretha – Gandhi was a nonviolent leader in India who succeeded in proving that the English people discriminated against the Indians' rights while they were in their own country.

Mai – You mean real Indians?

Aretha – Yep, people born and raised in India are called Indians, not the so-called Native American Indians that Christopher Columbus named. The real Indians live over there next to China.

Mai – You are up on it!

Aretha – That's because Mr. Thompson makes everything real and connected. He showed us on the map of the world where India was. We saw pictures from Indian magazines. Martin Luther King got many of his ideas from other famous people. Dr. King acknowledged Mr. Randolph's contribution to the Civil Rights Movement in the 60s when they had a *March on Washington*. People said that A. Philip Randolph was the father of the modern civil rights movement because he organized the Pullman porters and championed rights for workers in other areas such as the bus drivers in New York. Dr. King also got ideas from Henry David Thoreau who wrote about Civil Disobedience and the need for Americans to take charge of their lives.

Mai – I'm beginning to see the connection. The American Revolution, back in 1776, was about civil disobedience and our need to break away from Great Britain and I think King George.

Aretha – Now you're getting it! Everything is connected. Thoreau wrote years after the Revolution but the connection is right on. History is just like that game where you connect the dots. Like some wise person once said, "If you don't stand for something, then you stand for nothing."

Mai – And like another wise person said, "If you don't stand up against injustices, injustices will knock you down, stomp on you, bury you, and then throw away your tombstone."

Aretha – Wow! That's profound. Who said that?

Mai Ling – Me. Little 'ole me. I figured that out when I started roller skating.

[They both laugh and walk away.]

I Love a Liar

[Act V: Scene 5. Carmelita and Aretha are seen in another booth in the restaurant.]

Carmelita – My boyfriend is always lying to me and I love it.

Aretha – Are you weird or something?

Carmen – Why do you ask that?

Retha – Well, most girls would hate their man lying to them all the time. You act like it's a game or something entertaining.

Carmen – It is. Girls who hate boys that lie don't understand men.

Retha – So you're saying that you do?

Carmen – Yeah. You see men are going to do what they want to do. Some will lie to you when confronted or caught. Others will try to weasel their way out. Very few men will be straightforward and tell a woman the truth. In fact, most women can't handle the truth; they prefer a lie. Lies usually sound better than the truth.

Retha – So if your boyfriend is doing something that you disapprove of, you are going to confront him and you expect to be told a boldfaced lie.

Carmen – That's right. In fact, I grill him, like you put veggies on a barbecue grill. I'm like Perry Mason interrogating a hostile witness. I ask questions and he provides lies. This continues until I am fully satisfied.

Retha – Satisfied?

Carmen – Yep, satiated with my lust for entertainment. You see, I know he's lying. I just want to see how far he will go with the charade. I also store up his falsehoods for further reference. I might need to lie to him one day, and if I get caught, I can regurgitate his muck back on him.

Retha – That's weird. You create a storehouse of his lies so that you can throw them back into his face when he catches you in a lie.

Carmen – Or almost catches me. That's the beauty of lying. You can be creative. If one lie doesn't work out, you can modify it and make it better. One time he caught me in a lie, so I then changed it totally. When he said to me that I had completely changed my story, I lied and said, "No, you misremembered it."

Retha – Misremembered it? Is that a real word or did you just make it up?

Carmen – It's a real word. I had to look it up myself when I first heard it because I was a skeptic like you; I didn't think the word actually existed. I heard a politician saying that word one day on TV. When the reporters questioned this guy about his past – it was probably some shady deal that went sour – the guy didn't provide all of the details about his past. I think he even manufactured some parts of his story. So years later, when evidence was mounting up against this guy and the courts had this guy cornered, instead of admitting to a falsehood, he said, "I apologize. It seems as though I misremembered it." [*Pause*] I thought that response was *so* cool.

Retha – Yeah, my gramps does something similar. When people try to corner him, he conveniently doesn't remember. He says things like, "You're probably right, it's just that I don't recollect." He blames it on Alzheimer's or having a "senior moment".

Carmen – Yeah, come to think of it, my uncle has a phrase that relates to his drinking. I can't remember the exact words, but he says something about blaming it on the alcohol. When his wife tries to persist getting him to remember something that happened or what he said or did, he replies, "I must have had too much to drink that day. I'm lost."

Retha – But I heard that alcohol can *truly* affect your memory. I think that it is a serious contributor to brain loss.

Carmen – Yeah, I remember something being mentioned in our Science class that said excessive drinking somewhat damages or permanently damages brain cells. So this temporary amnesia thing with drunks could be real.

Retha – Yep, and it gives them a real alibi for lying at the same time.

Carmen – Yep, but my boyfriend doesn't drink at all. That's one reason I love him so much. He doesn't do drugs either. He doesn't smoke, snort, or get high off chemicals.

Retha – Are you sure? Have you asked him? If confronted he will just lie his way out.

Carmen – Ha, ha, ha. Very funny! I know my man doesn't do those things. The time we spend together is precious. I can tell. I can look into his eyes. There is no evidence of drugs or alcohol usage. I don't have to ask him about drugs and alcohol, and you're right, he could just lie his way out. But he is clean.

Retha – A clean liar.

Carmen – Yeah, that's why I love him so much. I know his vices – his shortcomings. Nobody is perfect.

Retha – Does he ever tip out on you – you know – cheat on you with another girl?

Carmen – I'm not positively sure. Sometimes he acts defensive when questioned about his activities. Once he told me that he was going to his grandmother's house to cut the grass, but when I called his house and asked his mother if Arthur was around, she replied that she didn't know where he was. I'm sure that his mother would know if he was planning to cut her own mom's, his grandmother's, lawn. When I later confronted Artie about his whereabouts that day, he told me that he doesn't confide in his mother about all of his activities. He said that he *had planned* to cut his granny's grass and just neglected to tell his mom. Later on that day, I got a chance to drive by his grandmother's house, and the grass was sky high and full of weeds.

Retha – So did he lie his way out?

Carmen – Of course. He said that he *had planned* to cut his grams' grass. He didn't actually say that he cut it. His granny would probably get some neighbor's kid to cut it anyway. He was planning to go over there when his boys needed him to play basketball because they were one player short.

Retha – Player is the key word here. He's just trying to play you. His boys will keep his back while he's playing you.

Carmen – I know. I know. But that's what is *so* entertaining. He says one thing, changes that scenario when he it doesn't pan out, and then creates another. He can make a square peg fit into a round hole. All the while, I'm remembering this scene, storing it up in my storehouse of lies in case I need to throw it back at his face at a later time.

Retha – I guess I see your point. If he isn't doing drugs and alcohol, a little lying is a small price to pay for a relationship.

Carmen – Don't get me wrong. I would like an honest guy. But what if a guy is honest and tells you that he's a drunk? What if he tells you that he is a pot head or is on the down-low ready to come out of the closet?

Retha – Yeah, you just reminded me of one of my cousins. He's on crack or pot. He steals from people and then tells them that he can't help himself when he gets caught.

Carmen – Who does he steal from? He should be in jail.

Retha – He steals from his folks, his own relatives. When they realize something is missing, their first thought is him. They then confront him. Instead of lying and pretending that the house was burglarized, he tells the truth.

Carmen – Wow, that's whack.

Aretha – You're telling me. They have to buy new television sets, DVD players, laptop computers, radios, etc. every year.

Carmelita – Amazing, but like I said earlier, "I <u>love</u> my liar!"

Creepy Teachers

[Act 6: Scene 1. School cafeteria during lunchtime. Ernesto and Berra at seated at a table.]

Ernesto – Did you hear on the news last night about the weirdo teacher?

Berra – Naw, I never look at the news. I'm, always too busy on the Internet playing games, listening to music, or texting friends.

Ernesto – Well sometimes it may be to your advantage to check out current events. When I had Mr. Thompson's class last year, he would always have interesting articles from the newspapers for us to discuss. He made writing essays fun. He got me hooked on the news. If I don't watch the 6:00 news, I catch it at 9:00 or 10:00.

Berra – So you're a news junkie?

Ernie – Not really. I don't watch all of the news on every channel. Sometimes I check out cable news, but rarely, but then last night I heard about a teacher in an elementary school who got caught taking semi-nude pictures of fifth and sixth graders.

Bear – Semi-nude. What's that?

Ernie – Well, he took pictures of his students, but he told them that they *all* had to take off their shirts.

Bear – I assume you mean that the boys as well as the girls had to have bare chests. How did he get away with this? Kids today are not necessarily naïve. Somebody should have suspected something.

Ernie – You're right, probably under normal circumstances someone would have suspected that he was a pedophile, but in this case he pretended that it was a special school project.

Bear – What kind of school project? Did he tell them that they were going to reenact the original hula dancing that was done in Hawaii three hundred years ago? Was this a history lesson about the Aborigines in Australia four hundred years ago?

What kind of school project would necessitate the removal of shirts by both boys and girls?

Ernie – This teacher convinced them that there was going to be a special school photo album. None of the kids told their parents because they thought that it was a sanctioned school activity. You see, there was no cause for alarm. A school photo album is no big deal, right?

Bear – The nerve of this guy. He had a lot of gall. He persuasively convinced the entire class. No one objected. That's incredible!

Ernie – Well it's true, unbelievable or not. The State's Attorney's office charged Mr. Smith, age thirty-seven, with ten counts of manufacturing child pornography. He could get up to fifteen years in prison for each offense. That adds up to fifteen times ten years. That's 150 years in prison!

Bear – Wow! But how did he get caught? You said that none of the children told their parents.

Ernie – Well this creep accidentally left his cell phone on the floor in the restroom. A janitor picked it up and searched through the directory in order to find out who owned the phone. Searching a link to the owner's identity, the custodian activated the phone and found pictures of boys and girls without shirts on. They weren't doing anything inappropriate, but the janitor thought it was still weird.

Bear – You're doggone right it was weird!

Ernie – The janitor then turned the phone in to the principal and Mrs. Peabody was in the office at the time. Mrs. Busybody is her alias or aka.

Bear – Mrs. Busybody is always in the office. I don't see how she gets away with it. She spends very little time in her own classroom. She makes her teaching assistant and her student teacher do all of the work. I'm sure other teachers are jealous of her. She might spend an hour or maybe an hour and a half tops, in her own classroom.

Ernie – Well this time her nosy actions paid off. She informed the principal of a serious decline in the fifth graders' grades. Kids who normally received A's and B's on their report cards, got Ds and F's on their most recent progress reports. Teachers had previously discussed among themselves about suspected drug abuse, but there were no visible signs of abuse. Usually, when kids start with drugs or alcohol, there is some sign. Kids become more obnoxious, they are prone to fight and argue more, or they are more truant or tardy. After teachers conducted individual inquiries, there was no evidence to link the drop in grades to anything.

Bear – I'm beginning to see your point. In this case, Mrs. Peabody, aka Mrs. Busybody, came in handy.

Ernie – Yep, the principal personally thanked her for her sleuth work. Since the kids were being suspected of drugs, something else must have been amiss. He called each child into his office, one at a time, with each child's parent or guardian present, and asked who took the pictures and what the reason was. Some students were too afraid or traumatized to reveal the culprit, but four students specifically named Mr. Smith, the math teacher and the organizer of the student council.

Bear – You say that some of the students were traumatized?

Ernie – Yeah, Mrs. Busybody heard about the dramatic drop in the kids' grades. That's why she alerted the principal. She did her part. See, students' grades declined because they knew, deep down, that something might be wrong, but they couldn't quite figure it out. It was like deep down they knew something was weird, but the teacher assured them that it was simply a school project. Conflicting emotions caused them to be anxious and worrisome.

Bear – Did Mr. Smith touch them or have them touch each other?

Ernie – No, he took each picture separately, behind a white curtain. None of the children saw what the other looked like. The boys weren't shy about taking off their shirts. Boys like to reveal their six-packs, real or imagined. When a girl went behind the curtain, Mr. Smith told each one that they had to remove their shirts. If they were hesitant or questioned his motives, he told them that it is now the 21st century. The women's rights movement is over. Women are now fully equal in society. Women are doctors, lawyers, judges, CEOs, automobile mechanics, firefighters, police officers, and soldiers. He said that he respected their bashfulness and that's why he had the curtain. He said that before he posts the pictures in the upcoming yearbook, each person had the right to review the photos and deny its circulation if the student feels that the picture of them is not right. He made every girl feel beautiful and every boy feel handsome. Somehow, each girl was convinced to take off their shirts. He made sure that he did not touch anyone. No boy or girl was physically molested.

Bear – It was still wrong!

Ernie – I know. The girls who weren't shy were then told that they could pose with a boy of their choice. Again, no touching. Just a couple of pictures behind a curtain. He said that he wanted to prove that the boys' chests were no different from the girls' breasts, anatomically speaking. He said that men's chests are no more interesting than female chests, so he then took off his *own* shirt to prove it.

Bear – So now he has individual pictures of half-naked boys and girls supposedly for a school project?

Ernie – But it gets a little creepier or worse than that. In all of the individual girl pictures, the girls' legs were spread apart. He had a red box and told the girls that they had to place one foot on this box while the other foot remained on the floor. All of the kids heard these directions because he repeated it every time someone went behind the curtain. Mr. Smith told them that all photo shoots look for a "certain flair" in the participants. They had to look suave and debonair. He told the boys to put their swag on. He encouraged them to let their pants sag down. He told the girls to think beautiful thoughts. What was most inappropriate here was that many of the girls had on skirts, so when they put their foot on the red box, Mr. Smith could take a picture that revealed their little thighs and panties.

Bear – He was really sick. A real sicko! I'm glad he got caught.

Ernie – So am I!

Berra – And it's ironic that the pictures he was saving on his personal cell phone were the items that incriminated himself.

Ernesto – Serves him right.

Bear – There should be some kind of school newsletter, issued monthly, to talk about issues such as these.

Ernie – Yeah. Just as we are talking and becoming more aware of things, other kids should be alerted. There might be more weird things happening in the city, at other schools, and we should be aware.

Berra – That's right. I remember Mr. Zid told us one day in Social Studies that some weirdo dressed up in a clown suit and was giving kids candy on their way to school in the mornings. Then, if a certain kid interested him, this clown would grab and kidnap the kid, take him or her home with him, and do all kinds of awful things. When he finished, he would kill the kids and bury them in his backyard.

Ernie – So you're right. We need a newsletter to share stories and better prepare us for the future. You get a lot from TV and movies but reading first-hand accounts is beneficial also.

Berra – I agree.

Do-Gooder

[Act VI: Scene 2. Arthur and Richard are seated at another table in the cafeteria.]

Arthur – Richie Rich, what's up with Mr. Washington? He is crankier than ever. He looks like someone who had a broom shoved up his butt and then broke the handle off. He acts like a crab that has been recently stung by a scorpion.

Richard – I believe that your imagery is right on target. He *is* crabby and he *has* been stung, but this time by a two-legged scorpion.

Artie – What are you talking about?

Rich – Well Mr. Washington is always concerned about us students. He's always snooping around. He noticed that Keisha was repeatedly late for school. She always had unexcused absences. So Mr. Wash pressured Key about what was going down.

Artie – Who does he think he is? He's not Inspector Gadget. He's not either Perry Mason or Sherlock Holmes and he certainly isn't Snoopy Doggy Dog. Why is he investigating the private lives of students? This is America – the Land of the Free and the Home of the Brave. We have First Amendment rights here. I learned something in that boring history class.

Rich – He claims that students are *his* responsibility. He is truly concerned about our welfare.

Artie – Yeah, I remember now, just before grades came out last year, he went around asking all of his students what they thought their grades should be. After everyone received their grades, he then asked students if they were satisfied with what they got.

Rich – I kind of heard rumors about that.

Artie – Hey, those rumors were true. He would interrogate us, find out if we were satisfied with the grades. If we indicated our dissatisfaction, he would further pry into our affairs to see if either we neglected to do the required work or the teachers mishandled the situation. He even confronted some of the other teachers.

Rich – Confronted them how?

Artie – I don't know all the particulars, but many teachers changed grades. I do know of two specific instances where the principal, the assistant principal, or the head clerk in the office changed a boy's grades.

Rich – What?

Artie – Yeah, Billy did no work all year. He would come to school late every day. His first class was Math. He would be an hour late or more every day, yet somehow he passed Math and graduated.

Rich – That's illegal! They can't just change grades. Or they shouldn't. It isn't fair. You're telling me that someone who did *no* work and was absent from the class practically all year due to tardiness issues, managed to pass and graduate. That's defeating the purpose of education. The other kids see that. What about future motivation? Kids in this school have younger brothers and sisters. Is this their legacy? Once the grades are in the computer, they should not be tampered with or altered.

Artie – Well, maybe not in an ideal world, yes. The fact of the matter is that the grades were changed that were in the computer without the teacher's knowledge and Billy graduated on time.

Rich – Well Mr. Washington couldn't rectify that situation but he has been known to be instrumental in changing the focus in other teachers. I've personally heard him tell students, "That's not fair! I'm going to speak to someone about that!"

Artie – So he is our champion? Our savior?

Rich – No, I'm not going to go that far, but I do know that Keisha was always late for school, so Mr. Wash finally went to her house to speak to her parents about it. Keisha's mom is a real wimp. She's got this younger man playing her. They aren't married, but you know the deal.

Artie – Playing house, adult style.

Rich – Yeah, well Mr. Wash asked them what was up. Why wasn't Key getting to school on time? He wanted the best for his student, Key. He wanted her to graduate on time. To make a long story short, Keisha's pretend step-dad (quasi) was really pimping Key. This play dad also made her brother become a drug runner because Keith was under the age of thirteen. Now Key's brother is never late or absent from school, so initially there was nothing to suspect, but because Key was always running late and her grades were slipping, all of this dirt came up.

Artie – If Key's brother, Keith, was never late or absent, how did these illegal shenanigans surface?

Rich – Well, as Mr. Wash was talking to them, he casually mentioned that Keith always had this worried look on his face. He had this distant, anxious look all the time, so another teacher reported Keith's countenance and demeanor to the school clerk, so it was not really official, but a kind of "I'm concerned about this kid" report.

Artie – A teacher casually reported it to Ms. Atkins?

Rich – Yeah, Ms. Big Mouth herself, the official 'blabbergaster' for the school. You know she tells everybody's business, including her own. They say we don't need a P. A. system because Ms. Big Mouth will blab everything to everybody. If you have a secret and tell it to her on the first floor, by the time you walk upstairs to your class on the third floor, everybody will know about it.

Artie – You ain't never lied.

Rich – Well getting back to Keith, you see, there was no proof or evidence that Keith was doing anything wrong. Mr. Wash just mentioned it to the mom and the play-dad. The pimp just flared up! He got real huffy and puffy. I heard that he was so tense that the blood vessels in his forehead were popping out.

Artie – Man, that's serious. I saw that happen once with the school counselor. He got so mad at some boys that he turned red as a beet, no red as an apple or cherry, and he was rushed to the hospital. His blood pressure had risen to an abnormally high mark and he was on the verge of a stroke. They say that he could have also died from a heart attack if they did not take him to the hospital on time and had given him medications.

Rich – That's serious. You shouldn't let people get under your skin like that. If people say or do things that you don't like, then walk away or ignore them. Well, Keisha's pretend-dad didn't ignore Wash or walk away. I guess he got tired of being questioned by Mr. Wash and spilled the beans about Keith. He was ranting and raving about what Keith does is Keith's business. If he runs the street doing chores for people, then that should be of no concern to some public servant, a mere school teacher.

Artie – This reminds me of World History and the Spanish Inquisition. I remember that they would torture you so bad and for so long that people would admit to not only the crimes they were charged with, but would admit to extra crimes just to stop the torture. They would put you on the rack, which would stretch your arms and legs. The pain was insufferable. After hours of having your legs and arms pulled to the max, people just gave in.

Rich – I see the connection. It seems that Mr. Wash just wore them both out with his questions and observations. This play-dad thought he was slick because if Keith runs drugs and gets caught, he won't do time because he's a minor; he's only in the seventh grade.

Artie – Yeah, but his record could be messed up and he could go to juevy. And his actions are still illegal. He is risking getting kicked out of school because of a bully.

Rich – You're right. He might end up in juevy until he is twenty-one, unless he joins the army or something. His life could be messed up because of his mother's boyfriend.

Artie – Yep! But what about Keish? If her step-dad is really pimping her, she might not get away clean. You know there are a dozen STDs out there, and everyone knows that AIDS kills.

Rich – Yeah, that's so whack. So Mr. Wash gets wind of it and confronts both Keisha and the make-believe dad. The man tells Wash, "You do what you gotta do, and I'll do what I gotta do!" This alleged pimp then shows Mr. Wash the door. I mean, he opens the door and just looks at Mr. Wash.

Artie – So did Mr. Washington call the police or tell the school counselor?

Rich – I don't know. You see, there was no real proof. Key started to come to school on time after this heated discussion. No tricks on the street would admit that they had relations with an underage teenager. Key is not going to admit it either. Mr. Wash didn't have a tape recorder concealed under his coat. Whatever was said, was said, and lost in the shuffle. Mr. Wash got Key to come to school on time and improve her grades, and Keith didn't look any better or worse after the incident, but this victory came with a price.

Artie – What do you mean?

Rich – The next day, Mr. Wash ended up with a busted side window on his car. That cost him at least a hundred dollars to replace. A week later after he got it fixed, he came out of school and there were two busted windows on his car, the passenger front and the passenger rear.

Artie – Did Mr. Wash call the police and his insurance company?

Rich – Not right away. Only after he came out a week after this new incident and saw he had four flat tires. You see, the window damage was below the insurance claim. You know people have deductibles. I think my mom has a two hundred and fifty dollar deductible. Well, if a window cost $100, then

Mr. Washington couldn't file a claim. He would have to pay any amount under two hundred. I don't know if he reported the two busted windows. It was on school property so he might have been reimbursed. I don't know. But I do know that Mr. Washington called the police after the four flat tires because this was evidence of harassment and criminal behavior, but without proof or evidence there was nothing the police could do.

Artie – What happened to Keith?

Richard – I heard on the street that he stopped running. Mr. Wash continues to talk to both Keith and Keisha. Both grades and attendance have improved but Mr. Washington paid a price for being a do-gooder.

Arthur – Yeah, he's the best!

Hoody

[Act VI: Scene 3. Robert and Richard are seated together in the lunchroom.]

Robert – Mrs. Woodard must have lost her marbles! Can you imagine what that stupid witch did?

Richard – What's wrong? The most liked teacher in the entire school picked on you?

Rob – Yeah, and for no reason. I came into class, on time, and she started ushering me out. She was screaming and yelling about "No one comes in my room with a black hoody on! Get out! Get out!"

Rich – What did you do? Did you waste her?

Rob – Naw, man, I didn't touch the heifer even though I was tempted. I said that it was cold in this school. You know, you go to one class and it's hot as hell, and then you go to another and it's colder than a dead witches' tit. I told her that I'm not taking off my jacket. Teachers walk around all day with sweaters and jackets on. The Dean of Students walks around with a coat on sometimes, that is, a sport coat. Students in other classes have hoodies, sweaters, and winter jackets on while they are in class and this crazy loony bird is sweating me.

Rich – That's discrimination. Was she only picking on you? What about the other kids? Did anybody else have on a hoody?

Rob – I don't remember because she stopped me dead in my tracks at the door to the classroom. You know how some of these teachers are. They nit-pick. They like to harass us about every little thing. Why is she stressing me about a stupid hoody?

Rich – Maybe she thinks that it's gang-related. You said that it was black.

Rob – I wear black because dirt doesn't show up as fast as if it were white. And gang-related? What about all these kids throwing up signs and throwing down hands in class and in the hallways all the time?

Rich – You're right!

Rob – What about people whose heads are decorated with gang paraphernalia? Did you see bulldog's head recently? He has at least four intricate artistic designs cut into his hair. Even the dumbest of the dumbest teachers should know that he's representing.

Rich – I haven't seen him but I have seen other designs in boys' heads. I know where you are coming from.

Rob – Well, Bulldog takes the cake. He should get an Emmy or an Oscar for his performance. His head is so beautiful and he's not the only one. I saw some rough looking chick in the lunchroom the other day. I don't know her name but she had this Mohawk and on both sides of her head she had at least ten different designs engraved. It was awesome!

Rich – I thought that the school was supposed to deter gang-affiliations.

Rob – That's my beef! That's my complaint. I'm just wearing an ordinary black hoody and I get put out of class. I have to go to the Dean and possibly get suspended. They will usually just give you a detention if you display the right attitude, but that's my point. At least one out of ten students, that's 10% of the student body, is hardcore gangster. I know a lot of gangbangers but I'm not involved. I don't represent and they don't sweat me. These teachers ignore the true blue thugs because they're scared. They pick on people like me to get their rocks off. They're punk bullies.

Rich – What's a punk bully? Someone who picks on just punks?

Rob – Yeah, or basically someone who picks on someone because they think he or she is a punk and won't fight back. A *real* bully will pick on everybody. A hardcore bully will pick a fight with people bigger and stronger than he, just for the heck of it. He has to prove to the world that he is bad. He has to prove it to himself also.

Rich – So where did you go? You said that Mrs. Woodard put you out? You went to see the Dean?

Rob – Yeah, she didn't give me the chance to go on my own. This knucklehead called security and one of those Rent-A-Cops escorted me to the Dean's office. There were so many people in line waiting to see him. The Dean was irritable when he saw me. You know how moody he can be. He acts like he is on the rag half of the time. He shouted, "Why are *you* here? Take off that damn hoody!"

Rich – So what did you do? All you had to do was take it off to keep from getting suspended. Maybe even suck up to him to keep from getting suspended.

Rob – In your wildest dreams. I just looked at him like he had just lost his marbles. He didn't have to come down on me like that. People were eying him and me to see what was going to go down next. He could have asked me nicely what I was there for. He should take lessons from Mr. Thompson on how to talk to people. Mr. T. would have said, "Excuse me, may I help you?" Or he might have said, "Could you please tell me why you are here?"

Rich – Yeah, Mr. T. is so cool and polite. He should be the Dean or the Principal.

Rob – Exactly! That's why I then looked at the Dean like *he* was stupid or speaking a foreign language.

Rich – He is stupid.

Rob – Yep, he's got all those degrees and still he can't think.

Rich – So what happened next?

Rob – Well then the Dean said, "Oh, you must really *want* 10 days?"

Rich – He was going to give you a ten-day suspension for just wearing a hoody and not sucking up to him?

Rob – Yeah, and you know how these well-qualified tricks are. First, he'll say that I refused to take off my hoody. Then he'll say that I was insubordinate. Next, he will make up some story that I was disruptive to the educational climate and my rebellious actions warranted immediate attention.

Rich – Wow! Where did you get all of those big words from? You might be too smart for school.

Rob – Hey, I have a PhD in write-ups. I have had so many of them that I could write a rule book.

Rich – So you were going to get a ten-day suspension for just wearing a black hoody in school because you were cold. The teacher should have been written up. The principal and the engineer should have been suspended for subjecting us kids to cruel environments.

Rob – I agree, but the system is rigged in their favor so I just gave in. I realized that the Dean was crazy so I just rolled my eyes and took it off. I've been suspended so much and I wasn't going to let these acid heads expel me for stupid stuff.

Rich – Expel you? What's that? I thought you were talking about suspensions.

Rob – I was. When they expel you, or expulsion as they call it, you are out of school for good. No more suspensions. I knew of one kid who was expelled and he couldn't attend any public school in the entire state. He had to move to Kentucky or Alabama to get an education. After a couple of years had gone by, he returned to his hometown and got back into a neighborhood school. He then graduated with some of his friends. Expulsion is no joke.

Rich – How can these teachers be so thirsty? All this drama over a stupid, black, hooded sweater. There are guns, drugs, gangs, and many other issues in society. A black hoody doesn't even qualify as a threat to society. It shouldn't even be considered.

Rob – That's why so many kids aren't learning anything in big city schools. There is so much stupid petty stuff by stupid petty teachers that can't really teach. They want to enforce stupid rules but they don't do it universally or unilaterally. They nit-pick on some people and ignore others. I think students fight in school so much because they get frustrated and choose to vent their emotions out on someone.

Rich – I remember one day in a Social Science class when the teacher said school officials started to enforce dress codes because students at Columbine came to school in long trench coats. Concealed under the coats were shotguns and rifles that the boys used to kill innocent people in the school. It was one of the worst massacres in school history.

Rob – Yeah, I read about it in one on my classes and certain precautions are being made today to prevent that from happening. That's why we have so many metal detectors and police officers in the schools today, but wearing a hoody because it's cold in class is not the same as walking around the school in a long trench coat. Things are out of proportion.

Rich – That's what I'm saying. It's like overkill. These school people need to get their act together. We need to focus on learning, not dress codes.

Rob – I agree wholeheartedly! Take care Dick.

Rich – Man, I'm going to kick your goofy butt right now, right here! I told you never to call me that.

Robert – But that's your official nickname. Think of all the famous people who have shared your name. Richard Nixon, a President of the United States, and Dick Chaney, a vice-president.

Richard – I don't care if they got a Nobel Peace Prize. I'm going to knock your lights out.

[*Robert continues to taunt Richard*]

Robert – And then there was Dick Tracy, the famous fictional detective, and a comedian named Dick Van Dyke?

Richard – So now you think that you are a comedian. Let's see how funny you look with your front teeth knocked out!

[*Richard lunges at Robert. Fists are flying. Rob grabs both arms of Richard. Holds him and then proceeds to calm Richard down.*]

Robert – I'm sorry man. I was just messy around. Words or names shouldn't hurt. Seriously, I apologize. Let's not solve our problems or differences by fighting.

[*Richard's demeanor changes. He is not as furious as before. His arms are relaxed. He is not panting as hard.*]

Richard – Yeah, you're right. But you need to respect other people's views. If I hate that nickname, then you should drop it.

Robert – Yeah, I'm totally sorry. Can I call you Rick instead?

Richard – Rick is ok but I prefer Rich like Ritchie Rich.

Robert – Peace Rich.

[*They shake hands and embrace.*]

VIRGIN

[Act VI: Scene 7. *High school cafeteria at lunchtime. Seated at a table are Aretha and Tina. Neither girls are eating their lunches.*]

Tina – Girl, I saw Zach feeling all over your booty at the dance.

Aretha – What are you yacking about?

Tina – I saw you two. [*Tina gives Aretha a condemning glance.*] You were looking up in the air like you didn't care. You were just pretending nothing was going on.

Aretha – [*Apologetically*] Nothing was going on. He wasn't that close. We were just dancing to the music; getting our groove on.

Tina – Yeah, [*sarcastically*] I'm not 'Boo Boo the fool! I got two eyes and they both work. In fact, I have four eyes if you count my glasses.

[*Tina smiles, places one hand one her hip, points her finger at Aretha with her other hand, and waves it back and forth.*]

Aretha – Well I just wanted to style and profile and I'm not going on the dance floor with another girl. Nawh. Nope. That's dope. And so what if he got a feel, no big deal. I'm not going to do anything – you get my drift.

Tina – Yeah, well, I bet it was a big deal, the way he was stuck on you like superglue. And what do mean you're not going to do anything? You aren't still a virgin are you?

Aretha – You damn skippy! I'm not giving up my stuff to every Tom, Dick, and Harry.

Tina – Did you mean just Tom and the other words were added nouns and adjectives?

Aretha – What?

Tina – You heard me. Think.

(*pause*)

Aretha – Oh, [*laughs*] I get it. Naawh. I'm not giving it up, to be precise, Ms. Snitty Witty. I'm saving my stuff for my husband – Mr. Right or Mr. Almost Right.

Tina – But girl you are missing out on all the fun.

Aretha – What the heck are you talking about? Don't you pay attention in school? Think about all those Health classes. Think about syphilis, gonorrhea, herpes, Chlamydia, and the thriller killer HIV-AIDS. Yeah, I'm missing out on all the fun. (*Sarcastically*) What fun is that? Who wants to die an early death just for fun? My mother knows someone who spends more than $1,000 a month for pills. Can you imagine what I could do with an extra $1,000 a month? Get real. I'm saving my coucie for someone special like Gucci. [*Both girls laugh*]

You know most of these dudes, if not all of them, just want to get in your snatch and brag to their friends. Sometimes they take pictures of you while you are asleep and naked. They send the pictures to their homies and laugh and joke about you. Sometimes they dump you after the first hit just so one or all of their friends can get a sniff. Look at Marsha. She was dumped by Phil the day after Kim's basement party. She told me that she did it in the bathroom. The very next day Phil tried to hit on me at school.

Tina – Yeah, I noticed that he's got wandering eyes.

Aretha – Not just eyes, girl. His mind, hands, feet, his thang, and his tongue – everything wanders and saunters throughout the inner city and the outlying suburbs. But when Zach pressures you, you'll fold. All the girls eventually give in. Guys say things like "If you really love me, then you'll do it" or "Everybody is doing it. What's the big deal?"

Tina – Yeah, I've heard that old phrase. If everybody jumps off the Brooklyn Bridge, I should jump too. But that's not true. If everybody is jumping off the bridge, I might jump or I might not. It all depends on the situation. If there is a terrorist shooting and killing people, then I might jump to save my life if I don't see a better alternative, but if people are jumping of the bridge because some cult leader told them that the end of the world is near, then I wouldn't go along. I've learned to think rationally for myself and evaluate every situation. I don't just do what everybody else does unless what everybody is doing is the right thing.

Aretha – Girl, you got smarts!

Tina – Guys don't realize that you're doing them a favor by denying their persistent requests. Not only are STDs unwelcomed, but *so* many babies are born to unprepared teens. You're actually saving the dudes from daddy drama.

Aretha – You're absolutely right! Did you hear about Ty? He almost cried when his son was born.

Tina – He cried when Cynthia was in the delivery room?

Aretha – No, he *almost* cried. I was in the viewing room and he was in the delivery room. I could see his eyes getting all watery, but the tears didn't fall.

Tina – I guess he was really shaken up.

Aretha – This *is* his first baby.

Tina – Well then, he should have been smiling, grinning from ear to ear, and passing out cigars.

Aretha – It must have been tears of joy.

Tina – What the heck is that?

Aretha – I don't know. I just made it up.

Tina – You might be right. I remember Mr. Thompson telling us that a lot of knowledge is intuitive. We know many things instinctually, without prior studying. Sometimes school makes us into intellectual dummies.

Aretha – [*looking perplexed*] what's that?

Tina – Intellectual dummies are those people who do well in school but can't really think on their own. They can read and memorize information and facts, but they can't really think and be creative on their own. We can know things by just observing our environment. We don't always have to read and study from books.

Aretha – I don't think that dudes like being cut off, but it's for their own good. They may not appreciate it now, but down the road in life, they'll be grateful.

Tina – Sometimes that may be true. Many people today take life for granted. They don't think about or plan for tomorrow.

Aretha – I remember our history teacher talking about that. He said that years ago, I'm talking about two or three thousand years ago, people believed in the phrase "Carpe Diem."

Tina – What does that mean?

Aretha – It means "Seize the day." Make the most out of today because there may not be a tomorrow. Party like it's 1999!

Tina – Why 1999?

Aretha – Again, people thought the end of the world was going to occur. They thought that the year 2000 was going to be Armageddon. That's what some religious people call the end of the world. Nations might have wars and kill off everybody with nuclear weapons or natural disasters such as hurricanes, tornadoes, earthquakes, and such will happen all at once all over the world. People started to party like there wasn't going to be a tomorrow.

Tina – But you said that the phrase "carpe diem" is more than 3,000 years old. People partied back then and they are still partying. What has changed?

Aretha – You're right. Basically nothing has changed. The more things seem to change the more things remain the same.

Tina – You can still enjoy life to the upmost today, but you also have to still be practical and plan for the future.

Aretha – So true. I always say to plan for the worst.

Tina – That sounds so negative.

Aretha – Not really. You see, you plan for the worst and if the worst doesn't happen, then you're not bent out of shape because you planned for it.

Tina – [*with a look of amazement*] Wow!

Aretha – Yeah. If the worst thing that you can imagine does happen, then you're ready for it. But if the worst thing doesn't happen, then you're especially happy. You're happy that bad things did not come your way, and yet you are happy that you initially prepared for the worst. It's a win-win situation.

Tina – Awesome! You're a genius.

Aretha – And so are you.

[*The bell rings to announce the end of the lunch period. Tina and Aretha get up from the table and dump their trays of food in the garbage receptacle.*]

Yearlong School

[Act VI: Scene 8. *Carmelita and Padma enter the lunchroom and sit down at the table. Both girls take small bites of food, mainly nibbling, focusing more on their conversation than on the cuisine.*]

Carmelita – Well in three weeks we will have the entire summer off for vacation.

Padma – Get ready for boredom and trouble.

Carmen – You don't enjoy your summers?

Paddy – Not really. At first it seems to be OK, but after a while, I get so bored and depressed. I don't have a job and everything seems to bore me.

Carmen – I know what you mean. [*Nodding her head*] Even with cable TV things get boring. Like right now, we still keep up with the latest movies and our favorite TV shows.

Paddy – Yeah, and with the entire summer off a lot of kids just get into trouble.

Carmen – Why do we get the whole summer off anyway? My mom and dad get more irritable. It's like they worry more. My mom might call me ten times a day to check up on me. I feel like those people who have ankle bracelets on from the prison. I feel like an electronic prisoner. You can't see the jail bars but you can definitely feel them.

Paddy – Well my dad left us when we were very young. I was three and my sister was two. My mom has been providing for us on her own ever since. She checks up on me about twenty times a day!

Carmen – She never married or asked your grandparents for help?

Paddy – Nope. She had one boyfriend, a nice dude, but no one else. And both my grandparents died before I was born. My mom only has one sister and she is always making money – she doesn't have time for kids or time to help her out.

Carmen – So I see why your mom checks on you so much. You're all she has. I mean, both you and your sister are all that she has. She has supported you for fourteen years by herself. It would be traumatic if something happened to you. And your only aunt doesn't want to help out. That's strange. I would think that she would be there since she doesn't have children. Is she married?

Paddy – Married to money. She has no children and no husband. She has dudes but one of the major requirements is that they have to have more money than she.

Carmen – Wow! One would think that she would be lonely and would want to help out, especially if she's rich. I wonder why people are so selfish.

Paddy – Oh, she remembers us on our birthdays and on Christmas, but other than that she is practically non-existent. I love her dearly but I know my mom wishes that there was more assistance from her or from someone.

Carmen – Yeah, it seems like your mom is a lone ranger. That's why I feel that school should be in session all year. Parents need help. Teachers can take up some of the slack. We can get into so much trouble even with our parents checking on us ten times a day.

Paddy – Why do we have the summer off and other schools don't? That doesn't seem right.

Carmen – My mom says it's politics. Some teachers want the summer off to relax.

Paddy – To relax!

Carmen – Yep, isn't that a trip! My dad works hard in a factory and he only has a three- week vacation every year. The good thing is that he can take the three weeks in a row, take one week at a time separately, or just take a day here and there when needed. But there is no way for him to take the entire summer off.

Paddy – Yeah, teachers have it made. They even get paid all summer to do nothing.

Carmen – That's not true. I heard that they have to go back to school and take classes to stay updated on the new technology and new teaching methods.

Paddy – A lot of people have to take classes to hold on to their jobs. I don't see why teachers get the entire summer off. The kids run rampant in my neighborhood. They knock over garbage cans, break bottles, break into cars, rob and beat up people in broad daylight. Some even burglarize homes. If they were in school, there would be less violence on the streets.

Carmen – Yeah, I agree. Last night there were about ten girls outside my neighbor's house. One girl was arguing with Deadre's mother. Deadre's mom said that her daughter was in the bed and wasn't coming out. Now this girl wanted to fight Deadre at 10:30 at night!

Paddy – That doesn't sound right. Why did she have ten girls for backup?

Carmen – They were there for support or backup They were probably there just to witness her kicking Deadre's butt so they would have something to talk about. Sometimes kids have a camcorder and record the entire incident like a movie. They even hook up a series of fights and label them and then sell them on the street.

Paddy – That's my point. Now, if they tried that in school, at least the teachers would buzz the office and security would have arrested or suspended her. Having all those girls with her would constitute mob action. Schools are supposed to be a safe haven for children. In my neighborhood, if you call the police, they might show up and they might not.

Carmen – Oh, it probably all depends on the severity of the issue.

Paddy – Right. [*Sarcastically*] Talking and arguing in front of a house is not as serious as burglarizing or killing someone.

Carmen – Sometimes the po-po don't come right away for a burglary. My cousin's house was burglarized and he said it took the police forty-five minutes to respond to the 911 call.

Paddy – That's ridiculous!

Carmen – Yeah, and they came drinking coffee and eating donuts. My cuz was waiting outside his home in 90 degree heat because when he opened the door to his house, he noticed that everything was topsy-turvy. Everything was in disarray. He said his house looked like a tornado had just ripped thru everything. The couch in the living room was turned upside down, the cushions scattered about, all of his DVDs strewn on the floor. His refrigerator door was open and the contents scattered on the floor. He saw all of this when he stepped into the side door of his house. He was afraid to enter because the burglars could have been in the upstairs' bedroom or in the basement.

Paddy – So that's why he waited outside in the heat. I don't blame him.

Carmen – Yeah, but the police response-time was ridiculous.

Paddy – That's what I was getting at when I said in my neighborhood the police might show up or they might not. One time a neighbor was arguing with his girlfriend, I think she was like a common-law wife, and five squad cars showed up.

Carmen – Five police officers! Now that's overkill for just an argument or domestic dispute.

Paddy – Really it was more than five because most of the cars had two officers in them.

Carmen – Well maybe Deadre's mom called the police before she went outside to argue with this girl and the police never arrived.

Paddy – But in all fairness, the police cannot respond to every situation. People need to learn how to take care of their own business. If there is a burglary or a murder, then definitely the police should get involved, but a man arguing with his wife or a teenager that wants to fight should not be the immediate concern of the police. That's why they are stretched too thin. They are trying to be all things to all people.

Carmen – I agree.

Paddy – That's why I say school should be in session all year. These kids need something to do other than argue and fight about stupid stuff.

Carmen – But we've had summers off for so long. People have got into the habit of doing nothing. It's going to be hard to change.

Paddy – Schools started having summers off because kids had to work in the fields with their parents on the farm. They were picking cotton, harvesting fruits and vegetables, or performing other farm related tasks. Now, most people live in the cities and suburbs. Parents don't earn their living from farm work so kids don't really need the summer off to help their parents. That's the dilemma. We have an antiquated system engulfed in a modern age. Our country has changed. The way people earn a living has changed. Yet, the school system, with its summer vacations, has not changed.

Carmen – I see your point. And these kids that are vandalizing the neighborhoods, putting gang signs on peoples' garages and other stuff, would result in less crime.

Paddy – Exactly! Things are not going to change dramatically, but if kids were in school there would be less damage done to the neighborhood and kids could have fun in organized activities.

Carmen – But there might be more damage and violence in the schools themselves.

Paddy – Hey, that's why there are professional teachers, security guards, and other school personnel. They should want to educate us all year long. They should feel guilty.

Carmen – Guilty about what?

Paddy – Guilty that we aren't learning anything every summer. How many teachers have given you a reading book list and you just throw it away as soon as you get home.

Carmen – I usually throw them away before I get home. I ball them up and throw them down right outside of the school.

Paddy – That's what I'm talking about. Kids don't care about reading those darn books on their own. Education is fun when there are other kids your age learning the same information. If we could read and self-educate ourselves so well, then we wouldn't need teachers.

Carmelita – Or schools. Maybe if there were yearlong schools, students could focus on their studies and sports activities. There might be less unnecessary violence in the neighborhoods. People need goals to focus on and challenge their energies. Without concrete, positive goals, people will just act goofy and do stupid stuff.

Paddy – That's so true.

Carmelita – We need to figure out a way to get our voices heard.

Paddy – And change the system.

[Carmelita and Padma hear the bell, stand up, and take their empty cardboard trays to the garbage can. They depart and head on to class.]

Carmelita – Holla at you later girl!

Padma – Later!

Cyber bully

[Act VI: Scene 9. Mai Ling and Rachel in the cafeteria.]

Mai Ling – I was totally upset with Mrs. Slondite today, and I'm not quite over it.

Rachel – What happened? Did you fail a quiz or a test? She wouldn't give you any extra credit to make up your grade? I know how obsessed you are when it comes to grades.

Mai Ling – Ok, I feel you. I can get pretty obsessed about my grades. My grades are a ticket to my future. If you don't do well in high school, why would a college let you in? I don't plan to work minimum wage jobs for the rest of my life.

Rachel – I'm with you there.

Mai – But today I was totally upset because I told Mrs. Slondite that I was being tormented by other girls at school and she didn't do anything.

Rachel – What did you say? What did you want her to do? She's not a miracle worker. You can't expect her to be like that lady, Anne Sullivan, in *The Miracle Worker.*

Mai – I wanted her to console me. I wanted her to help me and rescue me. I told her that other girls were ridiculing me on the Net and she just said, "Where are the girls? Did this happen in school?" I said that the incident did not take place on school property; they were either in the public library or at home because it happened after 5 o'clock.

Rachel – I'm beginning to get the picture. The school probably has certain jurisdictions. I think I heard someone say once that there is a six or eight block radius for school authority. I remember two boys were fighting on the street about five blocks away from my old elementary school, and they were *still* suspended. They thought that they were too far away to be disciplined. That's why I think that there is a certain distance that is measured before taking action.

Mai – Well she said that the school has no jurisdiction about what happens after school hours if it is not on school property.

Rachel – So you were upset, but I guess that you will have to drop it even though you are still depressed.

Mai – No. I'm not going to drop it. I talked to Mr. Thompson. He is so up on everything. He told me that a person could still get suspended if they bully someone; it doesn't matter if the culprits are on school property or not. They could be at home using a pc.

Rachel – Wow! They could get suspended for doing something in their own home?

Mai – Yeah, he said that if students perform actions on a computer that interferes with the education of another student, then *that* is what is called "cyber bullying".

Rachel – Yo! My, my, my. You learn something every day.

Mai – Yep, he said that he read about a seventh grader who was kicked and punched by a group of boys. The boy had to be treated for bruises and bodily injuries in Los Angeles way back in November of 2009. He then mentioned the suicide of a thirteen-year-old girl named Megan Meir who was the victim of an Internet hoax in Missouri in 2006.

Rachel – You said a "hoax". Is that something that was made up or make-believe?

Mai – Yeah, a hoax is a trick or a practical joke that is played on an unsuspecting person. The problem is that the recipient of the joke doesn't know that it is a prank and serious feelings get hurt. This girl, Megan, was so devastated that she killed herself. Cyber-harassment is what they call it and it is now a Class D felony in the state of Missouri.

Rachel – Girl, people can be *so* cruel.

Mai – Yep, and Mr. Thompson then told me about Kick-a-Ginger-Day.

Rachel – I literally have no idea what you are talking about now.

Mai – He said that Kick-a-Ginger-Day was recognized on November the 20th as the day to beat up a redhead.

Rachel – Get outta here! This is a bad joke, right? You can't be serious?

Mai – I'm as serious as a heart attack. He said that there was a cartoon back in 2005 called *South Park* that focused on racial and physical prejudices. People with red hair, freckles, and pale complexions were considered to be evil and soulless. After watching the cartoon series, some kids went around beating up other kids who had red hair.

Rachel – This world is sick! People see a stupid cartoon show and then act it out.

Mai – Yeah, that's why I'm glad that I talked to Mr. T. Mrs. Slondite just told me to suck it up. She said that high schools all over the country, in fact, all over the world, have bullies. Bullies have been around since the beginning of time. She even mentioned some old movie entitled *Mean Girls*. She offered me no consolation.

Rachel – Yah, but I wouldn't be so down on her. She was telling you the truth. She was advising you from her perspective. Maybe she got bullied in high school and figured out that the best way to cope with the situation was to lay low and play it down.

Mai – That's exactly what she said! You two must be psychic and have some extrasensory perception into each other's souls.

Rachel – Now, now, let's not get overly dramatic.

Mai – Ok, I was just funning you.

Rachel – How did the girls torment you over the Internet, if it is not too personal or sensitive?

Mai – They kept making references to my Asian heritage. They put on *Facebook* that people with my background or ethnicity do well in school because we are obsessed with academics and we don't know how to be social. They said that the only reason why I'm on the 'A' honor roll is that I don't know how to get a boy and if I did get one, I wouldn't know what to do with him. They said things like if I did chase after a boy, I would probably trip over my own feet because my eyes are so small and slanted. They said *so* many cruel things that I don't want to repeat them.

Rachel – I'm sorry I asked. I get the picture.

Mai Ling – I could just suck it up and say "That's Life" and move on, but instead I think that I should report them. What if they choose to pounce on someone that is not as strong as me? What if they pick on someone who is like the girl who committed suicide? It would be on my conscience if I keep quiet. This is not so much seeking vengeance; this is more like righting a wrong and protecting the defenseless. We have to take a stand on some things. If we never take a stand for something, then we stand for nothing.

Rachel– Not only are you strong, you are also a genius!

Mai Ling – I don't know about that. I'm just a concerned kid.

School is too dangerous

[Act VI: Scene 10. Berra and Padma sit together in the lunchroom.]

Berra – School is getting to be too dangerous to attend.

Padma – You aren't kidding. The other day a girl threatened to kick my butt just because I looked at her.

Berra – Why were you looking at her?

Padma – I don't remember. I think I was looking at her outfit. It matched and looked good, so I was just looking.

Bear – Why didn't you just tell her that you were admiring her outfit? Maybe she felt that you were judging her and looking down on her. Maybe she felt that you were staring her down.

Paddy – You might be right because she gave me this *hard* look and said, "What the heck are you looking at witch?" She then retorted, "Are you gay or something, 'cause I'm not?"

Bear – So what did you do?

Paddy – I replied, "Nothing. I'm not looking at nothing in particular."

Bear – Did that rectify the situation?

Paddy – Yeah, at least for the time being. I spent the entire day looking at peoples' feet. I am probably a shoe authority now.

[*Both laugh*]

Bear – People are so uptight nowadays. She was just probably having a bad day or just looking for a fight. Some people start an argument so that they can release pent up emotions.

Paddy – That's sick.

Bear – You're telling me. People are mad at the world. Maybe something didn't go right that day for her. Maybe she wanted to drive the family car to school and her mom or dad wouldn't let her. Now, she's pissed off at the world and wants to release her emotions and frustrations on anybody and everybody.

Paddy – I'm certainly glad that I looked down. She was a hard-looking chick. The kind that your grandmother would say grew up on the wrong side of the tracks. She was the kind of girl that could flatten a dude.

Bear – You made the right move. People are getting beat up, stabbed, and even shot over stupid stuff.

Paddy – Yeah, like when Kevin shot and killed a sophomore right outside of school.

Bear – That was unreal! Here it was the first week of school and he goes home at 2:30, gets a gun, and shoots Frank around 2:45 in the freakin' afternoon!

Paddy – Yep, and it had to be about something stupid.

Bear – I know. Almost everybody is in a gang or is at least friendly with gang members. You can't really survive in the jungle unless you have connections or some type of affiliations. But to kill somebody over an issue or on some unclaimed or disputed turf is too much. Both of them were sixteen years old. Kevin has to spend the next years of his life in jail while Frank's life is over.

Paddy – How did Kev get caught?

Bear – Well, he shot Frank right outside of school, then, see he went home and got his dad's gun. He lives right down the street. He came back and shot Frank in broad daylight. There were witnesses everywhere. He even had the nerve to return to school the next day at 8:00 in the morning with his book bag, ready for classes.

Paddy – Wow! So I see. Witnesses everywhere. And he had the nerve to come back to school the very next day! How's that for iron balls.

Bear – What gets me is with all this violence, teachers expect us to focus and concentrate on school.

Paddy – My division teacher talked about it for a half hour on college preparedness. We had an extended division this week, so they called it "Advisory". Everybody was polite, but nobody was really paying attention. It was as if she were talking in the wind. We heard words but the message was lost. What she was rapping about was trite. It was informative or educational, but we weren't really there. Whatever she was saying was definitely boring. All she had to do was study the class. If she took a minute or two to read our body language, she should have realized that she was lost. She needed to shift gears in order for us to get the message.

Bear – Teachers are so lost. They don't realize that timing is everything. Sure, discussions about college are important, but life and death issues are far more important and tantamount at that particular moment.

Paddy – That's what I'm talking about. My history teacher tried to relate to us later on that day. She didn't harp on improving your GPA so we could get into a good college. She talked about violence and the need for people to speak up if they see something suspicious. But we know this already. This past shooting wasn't unique. It's not a one-of-a-kind thing. Death is an ordinary occurrence in my neighborhood. People dying in real life is almost as commonplace as people dying in the movies.

Bear – Those video games that we play are even more violent that real life.

Paddy – So true! But at least the games are just that, games, but in real life you don't get a chance to get a replay or reset the machine for another game after your hero gets whacked. Frank isn't coming back. That's real. He won't be going to football and basketball games. He won't go to parties or his prom. He won't get laid. He won't get married and have children. It's over and it's wrong that is life is over so early. And most teachers are so insensitive to our real needs. They want to raise test scorers so they can keep their jobs. One teacher told us that the *No Child Left behind Act* puts undo pressure on his butt. If too many kids fail or have low test scores, he might get laid off.

Bear – I can see his point. He has to put food on his table. He went to college for so many years and now his life is threatened. I can see the school's point too. If teachers don't teach and students don't learn, then the teachers should be let go.

Paddy – Yeah, under normal circumstances, but there are so many issues that are beyond a teacher's control. Remember Arlissa?

Bear – Yeah, her boyfriend got shot. He died a week later after being in intensive care for a week.

Paddy – Not only did he get shot; he was shot sitting in *her* car in front of the school minding his own business. She was in the driver's seat. They were just talking. She was waiting for her girlfriend. Arlissa was going to drop her boyfriend off at work and her friend at home. Her girlfriend was slow getting out of class. Some dude just walked up to the car, while Arlissa and her man were talking, and shot him pointblank in the head. That was traumatic for her. She may be messed up for the rest of her life. How is it that a teacher should be held accountable for the progress of every student when unforeseen, unimaginable things happen that are beyond the teacher's realm or control? Oh my Gosh! Geez! What is this world coming to? What is *really* going on?

Bear – My Granduncle Joe loves that song by Marvin Gaye – What's Going On?

Paddy – What's a granduncle?

Bear – He's my grandmother's brother. Some people might call him my great-uncle. I can't call him Uncle Joe because I already have an Uncle Joe who is my mother's brother.

Paddy – I see. Well, we know what's going on in the schools, the neighborhoods, and in our personal homes. Teachers need to let up.

Bear – Amen. Let up and let us live. All this pressure about ACT scores.

Paddy – Hey, don't stop there. What about all the previous tests that are so very important every year. Those tests may be important for kids that want to go to college ….

Bear – And important for teachers who want to keep their jobs ….

Paddy – But what about what is important to us? Life is short. People are getting killed right here in front of the school.

Bear – Violence is everywhere. Like I said, school is too dangerous to attend, but in reality, danger is all around us. It permeates every fragment of our society. A kid got killed four o'clock in the afternoon going to the corner store for chips. He got caught up in gang crossfire.

Paddy – And what about the little girl who was killed sitting in the back seat of her father's car while he was on his way to pick up cigarettes and beer from the neighborhood liquor store at 11 o'clock at night.

Bear – And the girl who was visiting friends at a block club party who spent the night with her girlfriend. She slept on the couch in the living room, when at six in the morning, gunshots rang out, and ended her life.

Paddy – And the boy who was killed because someone stole his bike. This young dude was about ten years old who just got this bicycle for his birthday. When he found out who had it, he beat up the boy and took his bike back home. A week later, boys from the hood retaliated and shot him, reclaiming the bicycle as their possession and the original owner of the bike, a ten-year-old innocent kid, died.

Bear – And the mother who got tired of hearing her baby crying, drowned the innocent one in the bathtub. And what about another lady who got shot in the arm while sleeping and her granddaughter who got shot in the head sleeping in her bed at 2:00 in the morning? Something about a gang hit, but the lady and her granddaughter weren't the likely targets.

Paddy – You see, violence is everywhere. Not to mention the deaths in automobile accidents and other hazards. You can't just drop out of school because of violence. In that case, just drop out of life.

Bear – You're right. But we have to think of a way to be more careful.

Paddy – Like I said earlier, this hood rat wanted to fight me because I accidentally looked at her. We must learn to avoid people and personal contact whenever possible. People are carrying a lot of excess baggage. They want to unload it on someone. Stay safe and stay away.

Bear – Yeah, but you can't really avoid people unless you're dead. People can mess with you no matter what. I think that it's best to be nice to everybody, watch your back, and just hope for the best. Look over your shoulders. Think twice, thrice, and even more times before you act and speak. Think of consequences before a problem happens.

Padma – Yeah, but the bottom line is – whatever is – *is*.

Berra – So true, but it won't hurt to be careful.

Insane Teacher

[Act VI: Scene 11. Carlos and Robert sit down at a lunchroom table at school during lunchtime.]

Carlos – We had the most fun in English class today!

Robert – Fun in English? Don't you have that old, boring dude?

Carlos – Yeah, Mr. Sontage. He thought he was getting us, but we got him good.

Robert – Oh, so that grey-haired fox was outwitted. I thought foxes were smart, tricky and wise.

Carl – He wasn't as smart as we were.

Rob – So what happened? Fill me in. You have whetted my appetite.

Carl – Well, it all started out during the first minute of class.

Rob – You hooligans got wild that fast!

Carl – Man, we were off the chain. Mr. Sontage started the day off with his old, preaching message. It's always so lame. We just entered the room, sat in our chairs, and started talking quietly. You know how it is. We have different class schedules. When we convene in English, we have to catch up on the latest gossip. Something may have gone down in Math or Gym. We just need an update on anything new. Mr. Sontage looked at us with that condescending, superior look on his face and announced, "Look yall, I ain't having none of that nonsense today! We got too much stuff to do today!"

Rob – Are you saying that he *merely* said that and you and your boys jumped things off? That old dude says that same lame intro practically every single day. One time he preached about student etiquette, respect, and teacher abuse for about forty-five minutes. We had a double-block schedule that day. He talked on and on for the first period and we did very little work, and I'm not exaggerating when I say a little work.

Carl – Hey, it wasn't just me and my boys; everybody, well, almost everybody except the nerds, went off on him. Billy started it off. Billy said, "You're supposed to be an English teacher. What do you mean by yall?" Mr. Sontage then replied, "There's no need to make fun of my Southern background." Then Robert interjected, "He's (referring to Billy) not making fun of your background. He's making fun of your incorrect use of grammar. You're supposed to be teaching us English and you're always saying 'yall' and 'ain't'.

Rob – It sounds to me that Bill and Bob were right. Mr. Sontage is the teacher. He's supposed to set an example; that is a good example, a model of what is right and correct.

Carl – Exactly! But Mr. Sontage started to defend himself. He said that the word "ain't" is in the dictionary. He said that ain't *is* a proper word. He then said, "Y'all need to stop wasting time and start finishing reading this book."

Rob – What book are you reading?

Carl – I forgot the name of it. It's so boring. It took place about two hundred years ago. I think it was Tom Sawyer or Huckleberry Finn. I don't know for sure. All I know is that it is boring. It's like someone told you to look at the minute hand on a clock for the next eight hours. Then Donald chimed in. Don said, "We've been on this *damn* book since September! When the hell is we going to finish it?"

Rob – Oh, I know Don. He's a real thug. He can really go off on people. I heard that he just got back from a five-day suspension for beating up a security guard.

Carl – Yep, he's lucky that the principal didn't call the real police. That would have been assault and battery. He could have gone to jail.

Rob – You mean juevy. He's still in high school.

Carl – No, I meant what I said. Don is eighteen. They could have tried him as an adult and he would then go to jail.

Rob – I didn't know that.

Carl – Yeah, Don flunked Kindergarten and he failed the sixth grade twice. I think he failed the eighth grade only once.

Rob – Get outta here!

Carl – Yep, but let me tell you the rest. It gets better. After Don cracked on the teacher, Mr. Sontage's face turned red as a beet and then he said, "Donald, step out into the hall. I'd like to speak with you."

Rob – Oh, I've heard that same lame message a thousand times before. He likes to have one of those boring, private talks when he threatens to suspend you if you don't shape up. That stupid phrase echoes in my mind, "Shape up or Ship out".

Carl – Yeah, well you know Don. He didn't get up. He looks forward to a confrontation. Some kids wake up every day thinking about how they are going to get on the teacher's last nerves. I think for some students, their main job is to make the teacher miserable. They lie in wait, like a tiger or a lion, waiting to pounce on an unsuspecting prey. Don's eyes lit up. You could tell that he was energized. He just sat there and retorted, "I didn't do anything wrong!" Then Mr. Sontage said, "You cursed in my class. You interrupted the lesson. You're causing a disturbance. That's enough. Please step into the hall." Don replied, "I didn't curse. You're lying and making this stuff up. You're just trying to get innocent people in trouble and suspended." Mr. Sontage then said with his faggoty self, "Please step out, Donald Perrimore." Don said, "I'm not going anywhere. Take note, I *said* that I'm not going anywhere and I didn't say that I *ain't* going nowhere. I didn't curse. I used correct English, something that you must be unaware of. You said that the word "ain't" is in the dictionary and that it is proper. Well the words "hell" and "damn" are both in the dictionary and in the Bible. So now what!"

Rob – Oh, I see. He was live. I hate it when teachers get mad and then want to say your complete name as if that is going to make you do something or be afraid of them.

Carl – Man, it was *Saturday Night Live* up in there. The class was roaring. Mr. Sontage's forehead started to wrinkle up. You know how he does that when he gets mad.

Rob – Yeah, I've seen that. He looks like he going to have a heart attack or a stroke or something. His forehead wrinkles up like a dried prune or raisin.

Carl – I thought he was going to put his arm in the air like that guy on <u>Sanford and Son</u>. You know, the old guy who say, "Uh oh. I think this is the big one. I'm coming Elizabeth. I'm coming to meet you."

Rob – Yeah, but in reality, heart attacks are no joke.

Carl – You're right and I don't wish ill things on a teacher, but Mr. Sontage is a joke. He then said in a calm, monotone voice, "Donald Trevon Perrimore, this is the very last time I'm going to ask you to step into the hall. Would you like for me to get security?" Don said, "Bring them on! Hell, they are probably too scared to come down to this room anyway. You know what they say in the hood, don't start nothin' and there won't be nothin'. Don then smiled with an impish grin and the class went wild. Mr. Sontage was so upset. He walked towards the front door and Don ran to the back door. So while Mr. Sontage was at the front door trying to beckon a security officer, Don was at the back door entrance laughing his butt off. When Mr. Sontage finally realized that Don was not inside the classroom, I mean, not in his regular seat, he, Mr. Sontage, went back into the room because we were out of control and loud as hell. Don eased out into the hall, waiting for security. Mr. Sontage then said, "I'd like the class to begin reading silently, starting on page 132." Kathy then said, "We've been reading this book since September. Don was right. When are we ever going to read another book? This book is so lame." Mr. Sontage looked like he was on a very short fuse and said, "Katherine, step out into the hall please." Kathy replied, "Step out for what? You're going to try to suspend me for telling the truth? I didn't curse. I was not insubordinate. I'm concerned about my education. Whoever heard of reading the same book all year? Here it is February. We've been reading this same book since September. When I was in grammar school, we had to read a minimum of twenty-five books every year just to pass to the next grade level. Here I am in high school reading the same book all year long. Perhaps *you* should be reported to higher authorities. I'm totally bored."

Rob- I'm beginning to get the picture. I see. Now that Don was out in the hall, Kathy took the imaginary torch. It was like the passing of the baton in a footrace.

Carl – Yeah, and Mr. Sontage was so mad. He said, "Katherine, please step into the hall." Kathy replied, "Heck, I'd love too. In fact, why don't you step into the hall also? I was told that teachers should not leave their students unattended. [*Sarcastically*] I would not like to see you get fired for such a minor infraction."

Rob – Wow, she knew all the right words and the right buttons to push.

Carl – Man, she didn't curse. She spoke only the truth. Her words were not inappropriate, but her mannerisms could be interpreted as indignant and insolent.

Rob – What did Mr. Sontage do then?

Carl – He just looked stupid. He stood there not knowing what to say next. Then Kathy walked out. Mr. Sontage then said to the class, "Now I want y'all to begin reading from page 132 silently while I take care of this matter." Then Martha said, "I can't read silently. I have to hear my words." Someone else then said, "Me too. I have to hear my words too." There was still more chatter in the room. Mr. Sontage said, "Martha, please step out into the hall." She replied, "Oh, I'm going to get suspended just because I can't read like other people. That's discrimination. I'm special and you're not treating me like I'm special. If I can't read like other people then it's your fault. You're supposed to be the teacher. You have the word educator on your bumper. Why don't you educate instead of suspend. Maybe you should have the word 'suspender' or 'enforcer' for your bumper sticker. I hope you get me suspended because I can't read. Wait till my grandmother finds out. She will set you straight!" Mr. Sontage then said, "Martha, please step out into the hall, please." She replied, "Gladly" and stormed out.

Rob – So now we have three people in the hall waiting for a counseling session or possible suspension. Mr. Sontage is getting unnerved because he said the word "please" twice in the same sentence when speaking to Martha. Let's see – we have Don, Kathy, and Martha – all in the hallway.

Carl – Yeah, and we still didn't get started reading. As soon as Martha stormed out, Debra shouted, "Mr. Sontage, can I go into the hall also?" That's when the class went wild again with laughter. Mr. Sontage couldn't contain us. When he finally got a chance to speak, he said, "No Debra, there is no need for that. You have done nothing wrong." Debbie then replied, "Well could you please tell me something that I could do that is wrong so that I can join my friends in the hall. I've never been suspended so I'm not really aware of wrongdoings." Man, the class was laughing so hard and I was crying. This was *real* entertainment. Mr. Sontage said, "Please begin reading silently.

There is no need for you to go into the hallway Debra." Debbie replied, "It's so boring in here." Then Chris said, "She's right. This book is so boring. They even use archaic and inappropriate words. They keep referring to the black guy, named Jim, using the so-called forbidden n-word. You don't want us to curse in class but when we read this book, the curse words are said in our minds. That's why you don't want us to read this aloud. You keep saying to read silently. What's the difference? A nigger is a nigger." Mr. Sontage turned red again and said, "Please, Chris, refrain from using the n-word. It offends some people and is deemed inappropriate." Chris then said, "Refrain from using the n-word. It's used throughout this book. We hear it in movies, in rap songs, in the streets, and in our homes. What's the big deal! Is this book sanctioned by the school board or is it one of your personal favorites? Perhaps you like these stereotypes in books to demean us black people. You want us to read a book that has cussing and yet you don't want us to cuss in class. That's stupid. That's hypocritical. This is a stupid book and you're a stupid teacher!"

Rob – Oh me oh my! I know what's coming up next. Another one destined for the hall. How many minutes have transpired?

Carl – I think at least ten minutes have been wasted, maybe fifteen. No meaningful instruction has occurred. Mr. Sontage then said ….

Rob – I know, he said, "Chris, please step out into the hall."

Carl – You're right!

Rob – And Chris went willingly, right?

Carl – Not only did he go willingly, but he went dramatically. He said, "Yo, my nigga, I'm outta here!"

Rob – I know that the class went wild again.

Carl – Yep. Mr. Sontage couldn't contain or restrain us. We then looked at each other. No one spoke directly, but we had some type of mental telepathy. The message that was being transmitted was simply today is the day to clown. Today is going to be a non-work day. Arthur then shouted, "It's too damn hot in this class to read anyway! I can't focus on reading! It's about 100 degrees in this here hellhole!"

Rob – Why was he exaggerating? Just clowning around, I suppose.

Carl – No, this was serious. This was the truth. Here it was in the middle of winter, this being the month of February, and it was literally between 90 and 100 degrees in the room.

Rob – I find that hard to believe.

Carlos – I'm serious. If you don't believe me, ask any of the students that go to Room 325 or ask the security guards stationed on the floor. For some retarded reason, the engineer raised the heat setting. I heard that people on the first floor complained that it was too cold. He raised the heat so they could be warmer. As you know, heat rises, so the rooms on the third floor were like an oven on Thanksgiving Day. It was hot as hell in the room.

Rob – Well, it *was* winter. The engineer probably felt that all you had to do was open the windows to let in some cool air.

Carlos – That's what was so insane. We had all the windows open. They were open as high as they could go. We had six windows open. They were raised about six feet high. That's double what the norm is. They were as high as they could be and it was still hot as hell because there was no breeze coming through whatsoever. You know that there is a big office building nearby the school that blocks fresh air. It was stifling and sickening.

Rob – If what you say is true, then that was a safety violation. Somebody could have had a heat stroke.

Carlos – You're right. Asia asked Mr. Sontage if she could go to see the nurse because she has asthma. Asia said that the nurse had her pump or inhaler. She told Mr. Sontage that she was getting a bad headache.

Rob – She was probably lying. The nurse doesn't keep students personal inhalers. Asia probably left it in her locker. She just wanted to get out the room because nothing productive was being accomplished. Asia is an 'A' student. She was just bored.

Carlos – I agree. Well, Mr. Sontage must have gotten worried and he let her go to the nurse's office. He didn't have time for more distractions. He still had to deal with all of the students in the hallway that he put out of class.

Rob – So he had Billy, Bob, Don, Kathy, Martha, Debra, and Chris in the hall waiting for his special talk or a trip to the Dean's office for a suspension.

Carlos – Not quite. Debra remained in the class. Mr. Sontage then told the remaining students to read silently while he hurriedly stepped out into the hall. He then flagged down a security officer, who watched us read, while Mr. Sontage escorted six students to the Dean's office.

Rob – That's unreal! The kids were making Mr. Sontage look bad. It looked as if the teacher was losing or had just lost control of the class. He was trying to get them suspended and look bad when in reality it was *he* that was looking bad.

Carlos – So true! Well after about ten minutes, everyone reentered the room. People were whispering and asking questions about the details. We wanted to know who got suspended. It turned out that nobody was suspended. Everybody was given a warning. We were quiet for the remainder of that class period, but we clowned again the next day.

Robert – I bet Mr. Sontage got a warning from the principal also.

Carlos – You're right! They say, "What's good for the goose is also good for the gander."

Carlos – For real. He is really an *insane* teacher. He needs to be fired and never rehired.

Robert – Ditto.

Carlos – And Mr. J should get fired for wearing those same black pants and white shirt every single day to class.

Robert – Not the black slacks that are shinier than dollar store aluminum foil in the seat?

Carlos – You know it! And that dingy off-white shirt that has more wrinkles than a dried prune.

Robert – For real! Is that shirt off-white, light gray, or dingy yellow? Goodwill or the Thrift store wouldn't accept his stuff.

Carlos – Yeah, the green box would throw it away.

Robert – And while we're at it, fire Mr. T for that haircut.

Carlos – Oh, you are on it. He must go to Barber College with that look.

Robert – Naw. He must do it himself at home. He must have gotten Ray Charles to cut his hair. I heard some girls dissing him. They told him to his face that he must dress in the dark cause his clothes never match. He looked down and realized that he had on one black sock and one navy blue one. His other stuff had no color coordination either.

Carlos – Maybe he's color-blind. While we're at it, fire Ms. Williams also for those lame outfits. Every Monday, it's that same pink dress.

Robert – And every Tuesday it's the blue one and on Wednesdays it's the white one.

Carlos – Yeah, I don't ever need to look on the calendar, just look at her and I know what day it is. Like on Wednesdays, we always have a quiz in Physics and a test on Friday. If I forget what day it is, I just check out Ms. Williams.

Robert – Yeah, my mom told me that she wears the same black outfit every parent-teacher night. My sister, who is five years older than me, said that she wore the same outfits back then.

Carlos – But all kidding aside, we have some great teachers. They shouldn't really be fired. Perhaps they just need a visit from the fashion police.

Robert – Yep, cause Mr. K is the best teacher. I got an A out of his class and people thought that I was smart. They wondered how I got an A from Physics.

Carlos – You probably paid attention. I like the way that he explains everything, gives a quiz every Wednesday, reviews the material every Thursday, and then gives a test every Friday.

Robert – For real! He is so organized.

Carlos – Yep. I remember the first day of class. He put his name on the board and asked someone to pronounce it. Nobody could. It starts with a "K" and ends with a "Z".

Robert – Yeah, and I think that it has every letter in the alphabet.

Carlos – Yeah, that name is super long. That's why he told us just to call him Mr. K.

Robert – And Ms. Williams, even though she wears those same outfits every day, she is the best. She never gets mad or raises her voice. She is always polite to everyone – students, teachers, parents, custodians… everybody.

Carlos – Yeah. Teachers could learn from her, even Mr. Sontage. Maybe he shouldn't get be fired after all. Someone should tell him about his errors so he could mend his ways.

Robert – Yeah. If we are supposed to learn new things every day, then teachers should do the same.

Carlos – Wow. Maybe you should make a movie and be the director. We could teach the teachers.

Robert – Maybe.

[*Curtain is lowered*]